Helen Sandler's writing has appeared in various magazines and anthologies, including *The Diva Book of Short Stories* (2000) which she edited. *The Touch Typist* is her first 'proper' novel; her debut was the highly improper *Big Deal* (Sapphire, 1999). Born in Manchester in 1967, she lives in north London.

THE TOUCH TYPIST

Helen Sandler

*Author's note: This book was written before the attacks
in the United States in September 2001.*

Parts of this novel first appeared in a different form
as 'Modern Interiors' in *The Diva Book of Short Stories* (2000).

First published 2001 by Diva Books,
an imprint of Millivres Limited,
part of the Millivres Prowler Group,
116-134 Bayham Street, London NW1 0BA

A catalogue record for this book is available from the British Library.

ISBN 1 873741 65 0

Cover design and illustration by Andrew Biscomb

Printed and bound in Finland by WS Bookwell

Acknowledgements

My thanks – for inspiration, info, ideas and support – go to my friends, extended family, neighbours, and colleagues past and present.

Among these, and deserving of special thanks, are: Kathleen Bryson, Frances Gapper and my sister, Rosie Sandler, for their comments on the work in progress; Jay Prosser for Amy's co-ordinates; Sage for shared memories; Jude Barter for debate and reassurance; and, at Diva Books/MPG, Andrew Biscomb, Gillian Rodgerson and all the team for their enthusiasm.

Finally, I would like to thank my parents, Maureen and Phil Sandler, and my late grandma, Jane Tarlo, for their belief in me; Marie for helping me stay well; and Jane Hoy for giving me the space and encouragement to write this book, which is dedicated to her.

To Janie,
for the future

The Touch Typist

1
home

Modern Interiors

I didn't start off hating her. I had been warned but I was feeling kind of mad myself and it's all relative, isn't it?

I had come back to take a second look at the room, worried about the marks around the lock, thinking that someone had broken in recently – or tried to. I wound my way up through the house, knocking on doors to find a neighbour. At the top was a single door marked "Penthouse".

The girl who answered was younger than me, with a stronger version of my accent. She asked me in and told me that no one had been burgled but that people sometimes kicked in their own doors if they were locked out.

"The landlord's lost the spares," she said, as if that explained that. "He's a bit crap really but the heating's included. What's he charging you?" And we got on to rents in London and the imposs-ibility of buying, and my anxiety started to lift. She gestured around her own bright kitchen and told me: "He lets you decorate, anyway, you can do what you like to your flat – saves him having to bother."

Then she added, "I should tell you this, though. I bet he never said anything? The thing is, Joss, the girl next door to you is mad."

"What like?"

"I'll just say this, right. Ignore her."

"Why?"

"Oh, she's not taking her tablets and if you give her any attention, anything at all, right, like saying good morning and looking at her, then it can set her off."

"What like, though?"

"Just daft talk and insults. Just don't speak to her."

"OK. Thanks."

"Don't speak to her?" I wondered, as I ran back down the stairs, surprised to find it was only three floors down and not four or five. "We share a bathroom, for God's sake."

I let myself back into the room. Advertised as a studio flat, it was in fact a large bedsit, which someone had divided in two by positioning all the cupboards and bookcases down the middle so that one narrow half was the bedroom, which had the benefit of windows, and the other was a dim kitchenette with a little table. But it had potential. Even I could see that.

My experience of decor was limited to the past year's subediting on *Modern Interiors* magazine. I got into it through my sister. It didn't matter that I didn't know a pelmet from a finial and had to ask what MDF stood for. You could pick it up. And sure enough, I picked it up so quickly that I was able to answer "Main reasons for hanging voile at a window?" in the fun quiz at a company barbecue within weeks of starting the job. (Maintain privacy while letting in light.)

Being exposed to hundreds of pictures of attractive modern interiors, and writing advertorials for accessories that would look smart and stylish in any home, had activated a previously dormant bit of my brain – the bit that wants to liven up a dull room by painting a bright square of colour on one wall. (Create your own modern art for the price of a tester pot.)

It was a year since the breakup with Pascale had forced me into an unsuitable flatshare. Now felt like the right time to try living alone.

The girl from the "penthouse" upstairs and her boyfriend helped me shift all the storage units to one wall, where it became clear they'd been made to measure. Suddenly the room opened up to light and possibility.

You can paint white melamine units in bright modern colours after sanding and priming – and I did. It was while I was taking up the carpet that my next-door neighbour made herself known. She had been staying with her boyfriend for a few days, she explained, as she hovered in my doorway, trying to look into the room.

"Come in," I said encouragingly – I already felt as if I was lying just from the effort of not saying, "I hear you're a total nutter." She didn't quite believe the invitation was for real, and dithered before entering.

"What you paying for this?" she asked in a strong London accent – unusual in Highgate, which saw itself as a select "village", peopled by snobs, intellectuals and pop stars.

"Ninety," was my smug reply.

"Ninety?" she whined. "You're being done, intya, Joss? Bloody cheek." She crossed to the window in silent criticism of the high street and the traffic noise. Then, with a sudden childlike horror and delight, she cried: "What you doing with the carpet?"

"I'm taking it up. I'm going to paint the floorboards."

"You're never! Paint the floorboards? Why?"

"It will look nice. Like this." I fumbled through a pile of back issues to show her the full-page pic of a spacious loft apartment with its sunny yellow floor which dazzles visitors. (I remembered having to ask the artroom to flip the pic so the Purves & Purves wall clock was the right way round.)

Already I could feel the dilemma closing in on me. She was not acting normally but then neither was I. I was a nervous wreck, in fact. Her speech seemed strangely exaggerated but that might be my own patronising response to hearing a Cockney accent – where I come from, you put on that voice to mimic the banter in the Queen Vic. (And people down here, of course, do the reverse for the Rover's Return.)

I gave her a cup of tea and she told me all about her boyfriend. "Really he's like a fiancé," she said, and her pretty, rounded face took on a dreamy cast. "We're so in love, Joss." (This was the second neighbour to overuse my name and I wondered if they were all desperate for a sense of community, testing it out, or just reminding themselves of the name of the new girl so as to avoid future embarrassment.) "We'll get married, probably. That's all I want. Get married, have children. We'll have our own flat." Her face was glowing, her eyes big and blue and eager. "Everyone wants that, don't they? We're all only living here till we get married, get our own homes."

"I'm not," I said, feeling brave and honest and true. "*This* is my home." It did not sound brave and honest and true. It sounded false and pathetic.

"Oh right. You not got a boyfriend, then?"

"No."

"What are you anyway, eh?" I was about to say I was a lesbian when she added: "Are you an actress?"

"No… I did a bit of stage design at college… Why did you think that?"

"Think what?" Fear gripped her face.

"That I'm an actor – actress, whatever?"

"Oh, that." She relaxed and laughed a high-pitched staccato. "*Actress*. It's *actress* for a woman, isn't it? You couldn't be an actor, could you?" She laughed again and I felt we were spiralling together into one of those plays I never actually read in college – Pinter or something. And bizarrely, at that moment she was on her feet and pulling a Pinter text off the lime-green bookcase. I flinched.

"You've got all these plays, so I thought you was an actress. I was going to be an actress but then I got all my plays, you know, and I threw them on the floor; I took them off the bookcase and threw them on the floor and I took them to the cancer shop – they won't let me in there now and I tell you what, they've had enough stuff off me – and I thought, there now, that's the end of that."

"Oh."

"Yeah."

"So what are you going to be now? I mean, have you got a job?"

"No. Not now, no. But I'm going to work in the media. On a glossy magazine. But Joss, it's so hard to get a job. You don't know anyone in magazines, do you?"

I did not say, "Yes, by a strange coincidence, *I* am in magazines." (But I did recall the time my sister said that to the gasman and he thought it meant she was a model: "Now you mention it, love, I've *seen* you in magazines.")

By the time she'd gone, I was only fit to lie on the bed, go over every line of dialogue and ask myself if it proved her madness and if it mattered.

But I felt shaken. My boundaries – as a psychotherapist, a homeopath, a polarity therapist and an osteopath had told me in the last year – were fucked. They didn't all put it like that, but that's what they meant. I was supposed to feel myself as a channel of energy between the earth and the sky, gently close up the petals of any chakras that opened too wide, keep off caffeine and dope, exercise daily, meditate daily, sit up straight and eat fruit. I had started going to yoga but even there I noticed that other people's stuff was affecting me. If they lay down too close to me and my mat, their vibes started zapping me as soon as the teacher told us to fill the space around us with our energy.

New age spirituality and home decoration – I might have thought as I dragged myself from the bed and pulled it out from the wall to get at the carpet – twin voices of our age. Strip back to the bare boards and sit on them. As you chant, remember the tree that made this floor.

Bats

I hadn't known Madam for long when it became clear that, without my having said anything, she had twigged I was a dyke. Of course, she may have seen my books when she was looking at the plays on my shelf that day, or she may simply have guessed.

But her response was the same as for many straight people – she wanted to introduce me to the one other lesbian she knew. In this case, however, not only did she barely know me, but she barely knew the other party.

"Have you seen that girl?" she asked one day when she'd knocked on my door for no good reason.

"Which girl?"

"I see her all the time. In the park. You should say hello to her. You'd like her. She's very nice, very friendly. And nice looking. Bit like you. D'you know what I mean?"

It wasn't a figure of speech – she was checking I'd understood her code. I nodded.

"Go and talk to her. She's there most days."

"What time?" I asked, trying to find a loophole in the plan.

"All the time. She works there! Near the bird home. She's called Jennifer – it says so on her badge. She's lovely."

*

I had a polarity appointment later that week at 11. (I'd told my boss, Tim, that I was seeing the GP, because it sounded better.) So instead of my usual rush to work, I went to the café in the park and drank a coffee in the summer air. Then I remembered about Jennifer and asked for her at the sanctuary – a set of giant cages full of dying birds. I was told she didn't work there, she worked for the council and I might find her in the rangers' building.

By now I felt I was on an adventure. I was strangely elated and particularly pleased not only to be avoiding the office of *Modern Interiors* but to be looking down on it from the great height of the park – I could see the ugly grey tower of Magazineland plc sticking up next to the river, miles below me.

So I went and found Jennifer. She was wearing a green ranger's uniform and the badge, putting a collection of dead bats in order. "We had a bat walk last night," she explained. I wondered if this was the spoils or if she walked these same dead specimens around the park every full moon. "What can I do for you?"

I was not convinced she was a lesbian, with her long dark curls and that bluff friendly tone that outdoorswomen use to everyone. We hadn't immediately made a special lesbian connection.

"Er… tell me about bats?" I laughed to show this was a joke.

She laughed too – a sweet, relaxed laugh – and tucked her curls behind her ear before pointing at a spooky little creature like a winged black mouse in a box. "That's a pipistrelle," she said. "You'll have to come on the next walk. We show these to the children first and then we go in search of the real live things, with our bat detectors. Someone came along from the Bat Preservation Society last night – and a presenter from Radio Five Live."

"So they need preserving?"

"Yes."

"But not usually in boxes?"

"No." She smiled. "Why were you asking for me?"

I told her that my neighbour had suggested I come and say hello. It sounded odd. Then I added, "I'm quite worried about her actually and I thought you might have a better idea what's wrong with her."

This was perfect. It was a bit of a lie but it was bound to stir the heart of a caring professional, even if she cared for pipistrelles instead of people.

I saw her eyes flicker as she focused on me properly and took in my cropped, greying hair and baggy menswear. I held her gaze for a second and it was done – we both knew. But I wasn't sure what clue my neighbour had seen in Jennifer, unless it was just the masculine cut of that green uniform.

Well, you can see where this is going. We had a good talk about Madam and agreed she was barking and needed help; Jennifer said she bothered her every day, nearly; I said she hassled me every evening. Then I had to go off to the polarity therapist so we arranged to meet in a pub near the park after work.

And when Jennifer came back to the flat after the pub, I fucked her on the floor with my hand over her mouth to stop her shouting or laughing or moaning and attracting the neighbour's attention.

It sounds unfeeling when I retell it: her madness, Jennifer's fanciability, it's like I was unaffected. But in fact I was affected very deeply, just not in the right way. Perhaps having her next door was getting in the way of everything. And she was getting worse.

First she had the boyfriend over – or *a* boyfriend. Instead of a romantic evening planning a family or a wedding, they fought so loudly that I began by wishing I'd encouraged Jennifer to scream the house down on our first date, and ended by realising in cold-blooded horror that he was knocking her all round the room.

I was just reaching for the phone to call the police, my heart beating uncomfortably fast, when the noise turned to something like consensual sex.

Next day was a Saturday. I like a lie-in at the weekend but I was woken early by them shouting. She turned him out of the house as an effing bastard (and she did say "effing"), shouted down the street at him to never come back, and then cleaned the room noisily for most of the day. The climax was some kind of demolition job. After watching children's TV for an hour while the bangs and exclamations continued, I concluded that she was taking the bed to pieces without a screwdriver.

That night she knocked on my door after 12 and asked what I thought I was playing at. As I was at my most harmless and passive (lying in bed listening to Simon and Garfunkel in Central Park, half-stunned by spliff, making plans for Jennifer and me to go and live in Skala Erossos where she would track dolphins and I would produce a Sapphic magazine in two languages), I wasn't sure what I was playing at.

"What?" I asked.

"Are you trying to drive me mad? Don't pretend you don't know. First him and now you, playing your music so loud, don't you know there's other people living here?"

The look she gave me was frightening. I said I'd turn it down, though I could already barely hear "The Sound of Silence".

Seven hours later, she woke me by knocking once again and telling me how sorry she was that she'd been "rude" but all her plans were ruined, her man a bastard, she had loved him so much and my music was just the last straw.

Jennifer seldom stayed the night. Partly I was avoiding intimacy but mainly I feared that my coping mechanisms around the neighbour would be put under too much strain.

If I heard my neighbour going to our shared bathroom, for instance, I stayed in my room until I heard her come back. I didn't want her to stop me in the hall and tell me all about a boyfriend who might or might not be the same one – how strange that he never called, what did I think had gone wrong? And I certainly didn't want her appearing to me naked as I was going downstairs, by opening the bathroom door just as I was passing and letting out a piercing scream.

This had already happened twice to me and I was not the only one. It seemed to be deliberate exhibitionism, used for/against anyone whose sexual orientation might mean they would like to see naked women, i.e. me and the two straight guys. Was it possible that she could distinguish our footsteps? None of us, in fact, wanted to see her naked. It was an invasion of our privacy. I had trouble understanding my own reaction at the time, but now I would say it was akin to being flashed at. She was flashing her whole body at me but then screaming as if I had gone looking for her, as if I had *made* her display herself to me. This seemed to reflect badly on my lesbianness, which was most unfair.

Then there was the whole thing about noise. If there was any sound from my room, then she knew I was in and might use it as an excuse to knock on my door, for a friendly or unfriendly exchange. I didn't want her to know I'd got off with Jennifer, because I didn't want her to know my business, to gloat at having matched us up, or to have any hold over my life. So I was particularly careful to keep quiet whenever Jen was around, and to insist that Jen did the same. And when Madam did knock, my blood pressure rocketed, my mind spun behind my eyes, and I forced myself to the door for the next frightening encounter, all the time trying to seem normal so she didn't ask what was wrong with me.

"What's the matter with you?" she might demand, spitefully. "You're all white!"

Her disturbances – which were probably fairly mild on the scale of personality disorders – created or encouraged disturbances in me that could not have been much worse if a known lesbo-killer was at the door. But I had to deal with it alone. Jennifer joking about hiding in the wardrobe, Jennifer running a bath for two as if the bathroom was a safe and peaceful zone... well, it didn't help. It just underlined the fact that Jennifer was normal, grounded, sane, and I was not.

She suggested I stop answering the door. "If you can't deal with her," she smiled, tucking her hair behind her ear like Carol off *ER*, "don't answer the door. Don't engage. She can always come and bother me at work tomorrow if she needs a friendly ear."

I kissed her friendly ear. "You just don't get it," I whispered, resigned to a lifetime of sane girlfriends.

"Well, what's the worst that can happen?" she asked as she drew the curtains (in the same blue as the bedspread and the floor, to create a feeling of unity).

"The worst? I'll tell you the worst. Because it's fucking happened, actually. The worst is that I don't go to the door because I'm too fucked – because, say, I'm crying myself to sleep because I feel so lonely and desperate..."

Jennifer looked lovingly shocked and I almost melted.

"And then she starts to shout at me through the door about what a nasty selfish cow I am and how I shouldn't expect anyone to help *me* when I need it. And I can't shout back because you've told me not to engage."

Well, Jennifer had plenty more tips but I just thanked her and sent her on her way. She lived nearby with a jealous ex, but that was her problem. Until the mice came – then, I lost the plot.

Trapped

I saw the first one almost as soon as the weather changed for the worse. I heard a scratching that I'd heard before. Stoned and paranoid from some grass that the guy in the penthouse had promised was wicked, I froze in my bed. It was 3am and I'd been dozing through dreams where the magazine came back from the printer full of serious errors that were clearly my fault – captions that read "Joss to fill here blah de blah de bollox Joss to fill here."

Now I got up and crossed the few feet to the kitchenette. Two glinting eyes shone in the beam of my torch. I shouted, "Fuck! Fuck off!" It scuttled along the skirting board. I threw a shoe. Minutes passed. Then a scream from next door and a man (what man?) apparently chasing it on to the landing while my neighbour cried, "On the bed! Bleeding hell, no! On the bed!"

This chilled me. I had to watch TV all night, including American football, but I also had to wear earplugs so I wouldn't hear the mouse if it came back.

At dawn I called Jennifer. I was still shaking and my brain felt like it had shattered into fragments which were whirling and reforming beneath my skull.

She, as usual, sounded breezy. She was preparing autumn-leaf worksheets for visiting schoolchildren, as she brightly informed me. She laughed when I told her about the mouse, and offered to bring round a humane trap, if I dropped off the spare keys on the way to work.

I got home that night to find Jennifer cooking dinner and playing Radio 4 so loud I could hear every word.

"It's too loud!" I said. Then, "Hello. Can you turn it down?" I turned it down myself. "Don't you know voices carry louder than music?"

"It's all right," she said as she took the five spice from the cupboard above her head. "I told her I'm here to catch the mouse and she told me to make myself at home."

"You spoke to her? Jennifer! She's not supposed to ever know you're here."

"But I'm here professionally."

"Professionally? You're not a ratcatcher."

"Yes I am actually. Ratcatcher, mouse trapper, squirrel tracker, bird ringer. You should come on one of our wildlife walks."

"Can't we just kill it?" I asked weakly.

"No." She dug in the pocket of the green trousers, which still seemed indecently defeminising on her. "Here." She thrust a photocopied sheet into my hand and smiled.

It was headed "The mammals who share our homes". It was a survey of householders, to gather data about the eating, nesting and breeding habits of mice.

Four illustrations showing the same furry funster in varying poses were labelled common mouse, field mouse, brown mouse and house mouse – or something like that, I didn't dwell over it.

"There's no need to kill them," she said as she shook droppings from a plate into the sink.

"Fuck!" I said, wide-eyed. "Droppings!"

"Didn't you see how Hugh Fearnley-Wotsits dealt with it?" she asked. "He had them spirited away to the shed by a kind of exorcist."

"So I heard. I've been hearing about how to get rid of mice all fucking day from my helpful colleagues. But if we're going to exorcise anything in this house, I can think of higher priorities than a mouse."

"Oh, I thought it was vital to get rid of it?"

"It was, but it's also vital to keep it secret about you and me, so she can't stick her nosy nose in our business, and you've fucked that right up. Don't you understand? I don't want to attract her attention!"

"Well, don't shout then."

There was a knock at the door. I shot a look at Jennifer and answered it.

"Sorry to bother you, Joss," she said as if respectfully petitioning at Number 10, "but I wonder whether Jennifer, the ranger, you know, whether she caught the mouse?"

"Not yet," Jennifer called sweetly. "They usually enter the traps at night."

My neighbour stared past me at Jennifer, who was now right behind me with her hand on my shoulder.

"Come in," said Jennifer. "There's plenty of food."

Of course she behaved normally over dinner, while I couldn't eat, couldn't speak and deliberately kicked Jennifer twice just for an outlet.

But then she surprised us both by saying she felt ill. "Do you think I've been poisoned?" she asked, twitching in panic.

For a second I thought of mice and poison but then I remembered the humane trap. There was no way to reassure her, I realised – saying no just made us seem like lying poisoners and even Jennifer saw that we had to get her out of the flat before she came up with anything worse.

"Stop being nice to her," I begged Jennifer when my neighbour had been rerouted to the safety of her own room.

"I thought you wanted to help her? I don't understand what's happened to change that. When I first met you, you said you were worried about her. Or was that just to get my knickers off?" Even this language was not in her nature and she flushed with confusion and embarrassment.

"I *was* worried about her, I *am* worried about her, but my therapist says I have to cut off from her because I don't seem to have the resources to help her. She suggested I refer her to her, actually."

"What? Who?"

"The neighbour. The neighbour to the therapist."

"And have you?"

"No! What will that do to my fucking boundaries? I spent the rest of the session asking what she was thinking of and she finally admitted she'd just said the wrong thing by accident."

"Well, isn't she seeing anyone?"

"She's meant to see some shrink at the Whittington according to everyone else."

"Who's everyone else?"

"Oh, the greengrocer, the woman in the bookshop, and the landlord. I'm surprised you don't know, when everyone else in the village does. Funny how small London gets when you've got a nutter to share."

"I haven't asked her about treatment. It seemed tactless."

"Well, I asked her why she didn't get a better counsellor or something and she laughed and said why didn't I give her some cash and she'd go and see Susie bleeding Orbach. I was surprised she'd heard of her."

"Why?"

"Because I'm a patronising middle-class git. Take off your uniform, I need to relieve my bourgeois stress on your tanned and muscled gamekeeper's body."

We were woken at three by the trap snapping shut. Jennifer thought it was exciting. She whooped. She picked it up and told me with delight that she could feel the little mouse trying to move about inside the box. She wanted me to hold it but I told her to fuck off, with more sincerity than I'd used since June, when a man waiting for the nightbus asked to pinch my nose.

She made me get in the car with her and she unlocked the park gates and drove to the other end. Apparently mice will return home within a certain distance. Then she released the little fucker. Then she attempted to seduce me with bats flying overhead. She failed.

What the mouse saw

He was born under the floorboards and he followed his mother along the walls. There were different places you could go: the place that smelled of mice or the place that smelled too clean. Sometimes the places changed. Also you could go up and then there were more places but also cats.

It was best to wait till dark but if you couldn't wait then just run faster. It was best if they were quiet but if they had the noise and you couldn't wait then just run faster. Sometimes they would try to catch you. Then also run faster.

His mother had things she did and he had to copy them and if his thoughts made words then these were they:

Always smell before you go.

Chocolate and cheese before bed.

Piss in the cupboard, shit on the side.

Boundaries

After the trapping, Jennifer thought her work was done. She went to Lanzarote on an exchange visit. Something to do with a volcano.

Unfortunately it was not the only mouse. When I heard scrabbling on the Wednesday night, I would rather have died than have to deal with it. Jennifer had left the trap so of course the mouse went in it and then I was left with the problem. I was whimpering as I carried it outside. I was swearing in a kind of mantra as I walked down the street with it to the park, in my pyjamas. I was crying as I desperately tried to shake the fucker out of its box and through the railings in the moonlight.

I thought I'd done it and pulled the trap back towards me when I saw the tail flick out. I screamed and threw the trap, kicked it under the gate. But I couldn't leave it there. I knew I would feel worse without the device in the room as a terrible defence. Tentatively, I reached my hand through to give it a shake from the closed end. There was still something in there. I banged the box against the railings till the damned thing fell out, brain damaged or dead from fear. Then I ran.

Back at the flat, though, I was less safe. It might come back and there were bound to be more. Already the kitchen area smelt faintly of mouse piss. I washed out the trap. I had not anticipated either the stench of frightened critter or the quantity of squishy droppings. With all the lights on (to reduce fear), I saw more than I wanted to see.

The mammals who shared my home were taking over.

I rang the council but the exterminator had flu and the best thing for me to do, apparently, was to bait a few sprung traps with chocolate digestives and join the waiting list.

It is not an exaggeration to say I lived in terror. The days at work were not so bad – mostly I pretended to be OK, though sometimes I went out at lunchtime to cry in a secret corridor, down the side of the Oxo Tower. But the evenings, when even if I went out after work to see a friend or a therapist, I would have to come home to the possibility of my neighbour's visits; and the nights, when the mice ran freely round the flat because I could no longer bear to set and empty the trap... Things were not good.

I tried to block the holes under the sink and behind the fridge, the places where the mice could run between her room and mine or just emerge from under the floor into the wall cavity. I dunked pieces of an old sock and balls of newspaper into a pot of Polyfilla and stuffed them in the holes, only to wake to the sounds of mice building nests out of newspaper.

I could not lay killer traps with chocolate digestives because I knew I could not deal with their little corpses. Jennifer phoned once but she seemed more interested in some prehistoric homes she'd seen in underground lava bubbles than my problems.

It didn't take four therapists to tell me that the mice and the neighbour were combining in a supreme test of my boundaries, but that didn't stop them all from charging for this wisdom.

What the mouseman sees

With poison, it takes three to four days. Most poisons act via anti-coagulation. This means that the rodent dies from internal bleeding. You are unlikely to find a dead mouse as they die under the floorboards or drag themselves outside. Any smell lasts only a few days while the small corpse decomposes.

He tells people all this if they ask. People are funny about mice. They don't want them in their homes and then when it comes to it they don't want him to kill them. People say to him, "Can't you make them go outside?"

He tells them, "Mice can have as many as 13 litters in a single year. Do you want all them in your house? Do you? Mice chased outside will walk right back in. Mice can get through a hole the size of my thumb, see, look, that size. They love to climb. You can't keep them out, you have to kill them."

Some people won't let him in the door. One girl keeps calling him out and when he gets there she shouts through the entryphone at him to go away. He keeps going back though. One day she'll give in.

You find mice all over but it is particularly bad in these properties that back on to parks or wasteland. Also houses that are not clean. He has seen some very dirty houses and he wishes he hadn't seen them, to be honest. He wishes that when he went home to his clean house, he couldn't smell the mouse urine or the cat litter or the filthy bathrooms of those people. Some of them are asking for mice.

Taking the piss

Madam took to locking me out of the bathroom. The first time, I developed a paranoid fantasy that she was dead in the bath and I spun it out all night. But I soon realised she was just taking the key from the bathroom and locking it from the outside so I couldn't get in.

I knocked on her door on the third occasion.

"Who is it?"

"Joss."

"What do you want?"

"The key to the bathroom."

Her face appeared, screwed up and ready for a row, thinner than I remembered and surrounded by a frizz of unkempt red hair. "Don't use that tone! Don't you speak to me like that! Who do you think you are?"

"I just want the key to the bathroom."

"It's not your bathroom, you know."

"Yes it is."

"It's my bathroom too. You think it's just yours to use whenever you like."

"Well, yes. When I need the toilet. Please don't lock it. I can't tell if you're in there. I can't get in."

"So what? Why should you get in whenever you want? You don't own it. I lived here before you. Coming here, looking for a fight – you need help."

I snapped. "Oh fuck off, you stupid cow!"

I went back in my room. For the rest of the evening, I stayed in bed. Intermittently she came into the hall to shout outside my door. I knew I shouldn't have spoken to her like that but it was an enormous relief. I felt purged of all bad feelings.

Eventually of course the mice came out to run freely round the room, under the bed and in and out of the cupboards.

I left the room without turning on the light, got on my bike and rode off to the heath for a slash.

She never hit me but she did hit the girl from the penthouse over a misunderstanding – Madam thought "penthouse" was a serious claim to a superior home rather than a joke about a small flat on the top floor. The word appeared on a letter for upstairs and she pounced on the girl in the hallway and it ended in minor violence.

Then it came out that she had been bound over to keep the peace since an incident in the cancer shop.

I was sat in the kitchen sink when she next knocked. I'd taken to weeing there to avoid the problems surrounding the bathroom.

By the time I got to the door, there was no one there. But the door to her room was swinging about in the icy draught from the hall.

I called hello and a weak voice answered: "Who is it?" Her perpetual response.

"It's Joss. Did you knock?"

"Come in."

It was the first time I had gone inside. I'd caught glimpses in the past, nothing surprising, nothing to prepare me for this. She was lying on a mattress on the floor, with a cheap 80s patterned curtain as a bedspread. The duvet cover hung at the window: too small, it was pulled taut and pegged to the curtain rail. The floor was uncarpeted and painted sparsely with what appeared to be a single coat of white emulsion.

Her face, once pleasantly rounded, was now painfully thin, and her freckles stood out against the pallor. The place resembled a Romanian orphanage but the ammoniacal smell was not piss but bleach.

"Oh!" I gasped. "Are you ill?"

A bony arm, draped in a thin white nightdress, flapped above the covers. "I'm not well. I have to take pills but I don't like them. They make me worse."

"What are they?"

"They gave me them at the hospital. Bloody buggers. I told them I was sick..."

"Are you taking them?"

"They make me sick. Can you help me, Joss?"

"I don't think so. You should be in hospital."

"Bloody buggers."

"What exactly is the matter?"

"I can't take them pills."

Empowerment. She needed some kind of empowerment – or so I thought, in an effort to shift the responsibility away from me.

"There's not much I can do," I said. "You need to phone the hospital."

"Phone's been cut off."

*

I called my mate Drew. She had offered to intervene and now I could see that professional help was what had been needed all along. I am not a counsellor, which is just as well for the desperate folk of the world, and I am certainly not able to prescribe drugs or psychiatric help to anyone. Whereas Drew, with her doctor's bag and her stethoscope and her white coat and her new Beetle and her reassuring bedside manner – Drew was someone who could help.

I called her and she came round. My neighbour, to my relief, took to her straight away. And over time, Drew would prove to be Madam's saviour: taking her on as a patient, persuading her to see a tame shrink, and sorting out better meds.

The underlying condition and its causes (an abusive father or father figure was my own analysis) might or might not be tackled, but she put on weight and cheered up. She did not acquire a sense of irony but she did stop swearing at people in stairwells. And all this on the NHS – with the right connections.

What the mouse saw

This mouse was not going to eat new stuff even if it came in a box with a picture of a mouse on the side and a mouse-sized hole.

Everyone else ate the seeds and kicked them around and took them to the nest. He had always lived here and he had never seen this kind of food before. He didn't like the smell of the stuff.

And then everyone was sick. They stayed behind the wall and under the floor; they could not eat. His mother squawked in pain and then she stopped squawking. The mouse with the longest tail was the first to give in to it, lying on his side and gasping for breath while the light came and went between the floorboards.

When his mother was gone, he ran away.

2
esc

Easter, two and a bit years later

What the campsite lady saw

"More friends of Dorothy?" Irene asked from behind the reception desk.

"Oh yes," replied the larger girl, glancing at her pal. They looked similar to each other in their matching red tops and they were quite possibly having some kind of a joke at Irene's expense. But she had dealt with cheekier folk in her eight years at the campsite and she was not easily thrown.

"They're in Field 11," she told the girls. "They've got a fire permit. One car and one tent, is it?"

"Yeah, just one," said Fatty. She was certainly a big lass and so were the others. They would probably want the full cooked breakfast at the caff in the morning, if they got up at all. They might be too busy with the gang of boys in 12 – they were bound to knock up against each other – or then again they might be the other sort, they looked it but you couldn't be sure these days.

She signed them in, gave them a label for the tent-flap and showed them a map of the site. "Which one's Dorothy?" she asked.

"Oh, she's coming later." They giggled.

In the car, their rat-like dog began to bark. Both their heads snapped towards it but Irene took no notice.

"This Dorothy can pay for you all as a group if you like, when you leave," she suggested.

"Yeah, it's about time she put her hand in her pocket for her friends," said the smaller, less podgy girl, playing with the label. "We'll tell her." And off they went in their Fiat, just big enough for the three of them.

Sausages

"Hey, girls!" yelled Clare, flagging down a familiar green car. "Give me a lift!"

The Fiat came to a stop a few yards on from the toilet block and she ran to jump in.

"You lazy buggins," Felicity chastised her in the driving mirror.

"Buggins? What is this buggins? We do not have this word in my language," Clare replied as she petted her friends' ridiculous little dog in the back seat. "This is good practice for you, Flic, because you are my designated toilet driver. This is now the official Wee-Wee Wagon. Oh, and hello, by the way."

"Terrific." Flic turned to her partner in the passenger seat. "That's good, isn't it, Ali? Didn't you say you wanted to spend the whole weekend driving round the campsite?"

Clare didn't have time to waste. "I'm glad I've caught you," she said, "because I wanted to ask you about someone –"

The others both laughed. Ali brushed her blonde bob off her face as she swivelled round to look at Clare. "Let me guess... would that be Drew? Yes she's single, yes she's nice, yes she really is a doctor."

"And yes, Ali owes me five pounds," chuckled Felicity, keeping her eyes on the long driveway as children in branded tracksuits ran in front of the car like Nike-sponsored chickens.

"God, am I that predictable?" asked Clare, but the other two were arguing as to whether the fiver was due upon declaration of interest or upon proof of "action".

"There isn't going to be any action!" Clare warned them. "How cheap do you think I am? Copping off on a campsite? I haven't done that since I was 13."

"Ten years must seem such a long time to one of your youth," said Felicity, "while to some of us, it is but the wink of an eye... Jeez!" She slammed on the brakes just in time to avoid hitting a small girl on a silver scooter. "Bloody kids. I hope none of our lot are here, I shan't be civil to them. Which reminds me: I didn't tell you what Charlie did to Abdul at break –"

"No talking about school!" scolded her girlfriend.

"Too right," Clare agreed. "I don't want to hear you two talking about your boring fucking school, or about anything other than Drew, please – and start now because we'll be there in about twenty seconds."

They were approaching a sign indicating Field 11. In the middle of the field were Joss, Jennifer and Drew, lying on rugs where Clare had left them.

"Another active lesbian sports camp," groaned Ali.

"We've just been waiting for you two, to have a game..." Clare broke off. "Er, girls, I think Bodger had a little accident." She hopped out of the car, pulling her thin green shorts away from her damp behind. "Ohhhh, you fucking mongrel! Shit! Piss!"

Felicity clearly found this hilarious: "Welcome to the official Wee-Wee Wagon! Tell you what, Clare, save us all a lot of trouble, get back in the car now, have a wee, we'll say no more about it."

"Yeah!" Ali joined in. "Who needs to go to the toilet block when the Weemobile can come to you?"

"I've already had a slash, thank you very much. But now I'll have to go all the way back down to the bogs and have a shower."

"Not if I get to you first!" Drew – quite the dude in her skate shorts and flowered shirt – had leapt up from her place on the rug and was coming at her with a water container. "You just need a good wash-down!"

Clare ran off, shrieking, excited as a kid but half-conscious of trying to sound alluring, and glanced back to see Drew gaining on her and the stupid yapping puppy gaining on *her*. Joss and Jennifer were cheering them on from ground level, while Flic and Ali laughed the hearty laugh of vacationing schoolteachers. But Clare didn't care. She would gladly provide entertainment for the whole campsite if it meant she had the full attention of Doctor Drew.

Breathless, she gave in, slipped, and fell on the grass. Then Drew was on her, sloshing cold water over her lower half. Bodger shoved his face in hers and licked away. Clare screamed and scrambled on to all fours, but when Drew grabbed at her waistband from behind and poured more water down inside her shorts, Clare couldn't stop laughing, making it all the harder to escape.

"Got to get you nice and clean now!" Drew insisted. "I think we should get these shorts off you, they may be harbouring doggy germs."

"Fuck off!" Clare screeched, and they rolled on the ground together, whooping and wrestling.

For a second, Drew hovered over her and they were still. Then they were on their feet, brushing themselves down, and Drew was offering to drive her to the toilets to clean up. And everyone else was giving the pair of them the kind of knowing looks that could become embarrassing.

The tension kept building. They had gone into the woods together to bring back logs for the fire and Clare could feel her usually pale face burning, and not just from the exertion. There was no doubt Drew was handsome, but she was also funny and clever and, fuck it, brave. Wasn't it brave to launch herself at Clare the way she had? Without a thought of rejection? And it worked: all Clare could think about now was ensuring she got into Drew's tent tonight and that no one else got in it with them.

Joss and Jennifer had their own tent, and Felicity and Ali had successfully pitched their new purple and green dome with the words Beaver Creek emblazoned on the side. Drew appeared to have a two-person tent to herself. Was that everyone? Another dyke had been hanging around earlier and Clare really didn't know if she was with the gang or not. Drew was purportedly in charge, was "playing Dorothy" as they put it, but she hadn't even introduced everyone. But then, the others all knew each other, didn't they? From college or softball or maybe both. And Clare had only been asked along because Flic and Ali felt sorry for her, alone and single over Easter.

Doesn't matter, doesn't matter, she told herself as she opened another beer. Drew likes you, all is well with the world. But it was hard to believe this when the others were slowing down into a drug-induced melancholia that turned them into slugs, crawling about the rugs and in and out of their tents leaving trails of spilt beer and marshmallows.

They livened up at dinner time, wrapping potatoes in foil and performing acts of daring with the mini barbecues. To Clare's amazement, even the miserable Joss came alive. She didn't actually do anything useful, but she started telling stories, anecdotes, teasing people, and the others kept laughing as if they really liked her. They let her take centre stage and her girlfriend, Jennifer, smiled at her like she was proud to be married to such a laughter merchant.

"Well, ha-ha," thought Clare. "You haven't spoken a word to me all day and I ain't gonna eat out of your hand now."

It was dark by the time they ate out of their own hands. They sat in a circle round the fire and Drew kept opening more beer bottles with her Swiss army knife and passing them round. The teachers prided themselves on having brought every condiment available. "Ketchup?" asked Ali as she handed Clare a sausage. "Or would you prefer mustard? Or would you prefer both?"

Drew positioned herself between Joss and Clare. "This Clare is a nice girl," she told Joss. "I bet you haven't noticed what a nice girl she is, have you?"

"I've been too weird today to talk, sorry," said Joss, inclining her cropped head at Clare with a rueful smile.

"Whatever. I guess I've been distracted." Clare was glad of a chance to let Drew know she hadn't stopped feeling her presence.

Joss looked from one to the other. "Is that so?" she said slyly.

"Hey, shut up, you," warned Drew. "Don't stir."

Then the Jennifer girl piped up. "Is she stirring again? She can't help herself. Am I right, Drew? Has she always been like that? She can't leave anything alone."

"You are so right, my dear. So right. Our Joss is the champion stirrer of the lesbian world."

"Fuck off," said Joss. And, bizarrely, she threw her food on the fire and stomped off to her tent. Jennifer sighed and followed her.

"What's up with her?" asked Clare.

"I must have teased her too much," answered Drew.

"You barely said a word."

"Maybe I'd better go and apologise."

"No!" Clare grabbed Drew's hand. "You don't go anywhere. Especially not to apologise to the most oversensitive dyke I've ever met."

"Don't be mean about her."

"I'm just saying what I see. Nothing happened, did it?"

Drew sighed. "No, nothing happened. She just flips out. She reckons she's got manic depression, but if so, it's the mildest case I've ever seen."

"At least it would be an excuse."

"Look, she's my best mate, so if you want to be rude about her, talk to someone else."

"Whatever." Pause. "But, just to clarify – she's a moody cow and you all put up with it?"

"Clare, do you want me to keep talking to you or do you want a slap?"

She returned the stare. "Both, please."

Drew raised her eyebrows, then looked away. "Hey kids," she called to Felicity and Ali, who were tactfully talking amongst themselves, "pass the mayo, the brown sauce and the Branston's, *s'il vous plaît*. I have a naked sausage that needs saucing up."

They kept up the badinage well into the night and were wrapped in sleeping bags around a dying fire when a gang of youths from the next field invaded, in cars and on foot, headlights and torches on full, dogs running alongside.

"All right, girls?" one of them roared. "Fancy a bunny for breakfast?"

The noise and bright lights, designed to flush out rabbits, stunned the girls just as badly.

"Stop it!" cried Jennifer, who had stuck her head out of the tent flap. "Leave them alone!"

The boys only laughed aggressively, their vehicles swinging round 180 degrees, halting, accelerating between tents.

"Come on babe," said Drew, her arm around Clare's shoulder, "let's go to bed."

Burn baby burn

A car was parking nearby and the lights shone through the canvas, adding a brief ambient glow to the candlelit tent.

"Who's that?" asked Drew.

"Who cares?" answered Clare. "More bunny boilers."

But Drew threw herself to the entrance and unzipped the flaps.

"Yo, babe!" she cried, apparently delighted.

"What... Who...?" Clare wanted to shake her, drag her back into their special place.

"Hey! Twat features!" shouted Drew to the new arrival. "You're late, you've missed the sausages, and you're sleeping in Clare's tent! Go!"

An unfamiliar laugh, some teasing from outside. Clare lay down and pulled Drew's sleeping bag over her, so relieved that her whole body seemed to smile and sing. And then Drew was stroking her hair and handing her a joint. "It's Manuela. The girl that was here at lunchtime and buggered off again. D'you know her?"

"No."

"Do you mind her sleeping in your tent? She was meant to be in with me but..."

Clare passed back the joint, wrapped a hand round the back of

Drew's head and just looked at her. It worked: Drew fell on her and kissed her. Clare let out a moan and Drew echoed it as their tongues met. The good doctor had her fingers wrapped in Clare's blonde hair, her grip making it clear how much she wanted her... Then her moan turned to a shriek and she broke away.

"What?" asked Clare, horrified.

"Fucking spliff!" shouted Drew, hitting at her shorts.

"Have you hurt yourself?"

"Yeah. Fuck." Her face crumpled in pain and annoyance.

"Hey! Hey babe, it's OK. Come here. Let me kiss it better." Clare bent her lips to Drew's thigh and kissed the tiny burnhole in the fabric of her shorts. She let her hand brush for a second against the mound of Drew's crotch before settling on her hip. Drew was making little noises... *like a child*.

"So, it didn't take long to blow her cover," thought Clare (even as she continued to kiss her way around those muscled legs). "One more impressive facade destroyed by my own attentiveness."

What had she learnt from her many encounters with women? Maintain a little distance and they will keep trying to impress for anything up to six weeks. Give 'em what they really want and you will instantly glimpse the soppy interior swirling about, as if you had admired a big, smooth, decorated trifle and then taken a spoon to it.

Drew must have sensed a change in her new love; she sat up and frowned a grown-up frown. Clare looked back for long enough to let her know this was important.

"Do you want me?" she asked.

Drew stiffened like a tiger.

When they finally emerged from the tent, next morning or afternoon or whatever it was, the others were in much the same position as the previous afternoon: the lazing position. Clare's limbs exited the tent one at a time; they were empty as if Drew had drained them of feeling and left them open to the universe. And the result was that Clare was dangerously and dramatically in love.

As the other women registered her emergence, they began to applaud. "Oh, yes! Fast work!" said Felicity. Clare felt strangely separate from them, a little frightened of how she would deal with their taunts, but her saviour was right behind, wrapping her arms round her and kissing the top of her head.

"Enough!" Drew said firmly. "Put the kettle on and shut your faces. Come on Clare, we're driving to the bogs and we're not taking any of these uncivilised louts with us."

As Clare followed her to the new-edition silver Beetle, she was aware of money changing hands once again between her friends and another argument about the precise terms of someone's wager.

"Sad," she muttered.

"Wozzat?"

"Nothing. Just what you said: they're uncivilised louts."

"Whereas we are the most refined of gay ladies," laughed Drew.

"Wanna see me sit on the gearstick?" asked Clare.

"Mmm, that's what I mean. It's that kind of refined behaviour that drew me to you all those weeks ago when I first set eyes on you."

"It's nice of you to say so, dear, but you first saw me about –" she looked at her watch "– shit, a full 24 hours ago."

"Not so, my sweet. I first saw you at a party you may not recall attending. A certain fairies and elves party at which you were a little the worse for Pixie Punch and I drove you home."

"You what?"

"True."

"You manipulative bastard! You fixed this whole thing!"

Drew feigned indignation. "If you are suggesting I may have mentioned to Felicity and Ali that it would be nice if they invited you along this weekend... then you are making one hell of an accusation, lady."

"Stop the car."

"What?"

"Stop the fucking car."

She did.

Clare clambered over the gearstick and straddled the driver, grabbing her shoulders. "Don't ever lie to me again," she hissed, her eyes a centimetre from Drew's. "Don't ever, ever lie to me again. OK?"

"I'm not sure I've lied, as such."

"I'm sure you fucking have. If you don't know the difference, we can stop right now."

"OK, OK! I promise not to lie or to, er, be a manipulative bastard. But I don't need to, now, do I?" Drew ran her thumb over Clare's left nipple. "Because I've got you, haven't I?"

"Don't count on it, sweetheart. Don't count on anything."

They disengaged and drove on in silence.

Void

"What do you think to her?" Drew asked Joss later as they lazed in the sun.

"Who? That little slip of a thing? Does it matter what I think?" She followed her friend's gaze down the field to where Jennifer was bowling a tennis ball at Clare's outstretched bat while the teachers spread themselves around the place. It was hard to say who was on which team. "You have a new doll! So young and so blonde and so cute. Look how its little head moves when it sees you. Ahhh, it loves you."

"Hey, easy, tiger! What's going on?"

"Nothing. You asked what I think and I'm telling you. I'm congratulating you on your conquest."

"I really like her. What is it? What's wrong with her?"

"Apart from her cynical pursuit of you? Nothing."

"Eh? It was me that lured *her* here under false pretences, remember."

"Yeah, but look how she's behaving."

"I think it's called flirting, dear. She flirted a bit, I flirted a bit, we snogged, we shagged –"

"And now you're in love. Take my mobile – call Pickfords."

"Joss, for fuck's sake! What's the matter?"

"I am unhappy in love and I can't bear to see you happy. Skin up."

"Really?"

"Yeah, your stuff is stronger than mine."

"I mean, really unhappy?"

"Well, why don't you return the favour?" Joss performed a stagey clearing of the throat. "Ahem. Drew, what do you think of Jennifer?"

"Oh Christ, you know what I think. I think she's amazing and I think you don't appreciate her and I think it's time you looked at what you've got."

"Well, I'm looking and I ain't seeing it. We'll have been together three years this summer, can you believe it? To everyone else it must look like this nice solid relationship, but she doesn't..."

"What?"

"She doesn't fill the gaping void." Joss raised her eyebrows, a trick that (combined with the trademark ironic hyperbole) her friend recognised as a way of stifling the tears. "I don't feel held. That's it in the end. That's what I want all the fucking time and that's what no one can give me. I might as well be single my whole life."

"Whoa!" Drew patted her on the arm, uncomfortable. "Come on, that's the smoke talking. Jesus, she holds you, doesn't she?"

"Oh yes. She hugs me and she kisses me and we make sweet love and all the time I'm just thinking how I need her to fill the hole in my heart, the fucking big black hole. Sometimes when I think about her, I have a twinge of that in-love thing, you know? But when we meet up, I can't... I can't... I don't know if she's the right person and I don't know if it's just 'cos there's something wrong with me."

"Look, we all get that. But the thing about being a dyke is that girls like to hold each other. It's biologically determined. Girls hold. And without babies, dykes hold all the more. They're queuing up to hold on tight to you, Joss. Don't worry about it, just sink into her arms and let yourself go. As long as you do the same for her, you'll have her forever. That's where you went wrong with Pascale, you know. You weren't looking after her properly –"

"Sorry, can I stop you there, Doc? a) What kind of reactionary bollocks are you talking and b) how did we get to Pascale? Leave off Pascale."

"What's reactionary?"

"What's reactionary? Well, *I* am not biologically determined to hold. What is that about? Programmed to cuddle a lickle baby? I'd better stay at home and breed then."

"Might do you some good."

"Are you going to explain yourself?"

"Yeah, yeah, let's examine my politics and then we won't need to look too close at how you conduct your bloody relationships. Well, don't fuck this one up. That's your pattern, isn't it? You can set it up but you can't follow through. I know you. You don't *really* think you'd be better off single, you think you'd be better off with someone else, some fantasy girl you've got in your mind." She shook her head. "She don't exist, mate. Just get on with it."

"Ha! That's good advice, Doctor, thank you. If I can just re-member that, I'll be fine. Yeah. Just get on with it. You know, I feel less worried already. Oh, the hole in my heart has closed up. Look at the trees, look at the cute lickle puppy running around. Isn't life wonderful?"

Drew glanced up from her spliff-building. "You are a pain in the arse. No one made you come out here. If you don't like it, go home."

"Ooooh, snotty. Actually, *you* made me come out here."

"And is it so terrible? I just want to cheer you up a bit but you're determined not to be happy."

"Yeah, biologically determined." Joss swotted at a fly, then gazed downfield.

Drew ran her tongue professionally along the joined-up Rizlas and put her thumbs to work on the rolling motion before giving a twist to the end. Pleasing. Then she fired up, and dragged her mind back to the state of her pal. "Why don't you do any of the things you're good at, anyway?" she asked her.

"What? Where did that come from?"

"Well, many people find they're happier if they do things they're good at, you know, their fucking talents?" It was hard to hide her irritation at Joss's blocking tactics – and she'd just failed.

"Oh, fucking talents. That's your department, isn't it?"

Drew looked at her, willing her to talk sense. "I thought you took that studio flat because of the light," she said finally. "I thought you were going to paint."

"You what? I never said that."

"You said the light was good."

"I meant it wasn't a dark shithole like some of the dumps I'd seen. I never said I was going to paint. How could I live in one room and paint in it too? Did the word 'studio' confuse you, dear?"

They missed a beat while Drew took a long and audible toke.

"And I've got that nutter next door," Joss added, by way of an excuse.

It was ignored. "Has she even seen your work?"

"What?"

In frustration, Drew gave her friend a shove. "Stop saying

'what'. I'm trying to help you. You know very well what I'm talking about: have you shown Jennifer your paintings?"

"I barely know the girl. I haven't even shown her my verruca."

Drew handed over the spliff. "Here, take some more drugs," she muttered as she got to her feet. Then she turned her back and yelled to the ball-game: "Hold 'em at bay till I get there, girls! I'm coming in to bat."

"Hey, hey, Drewwww! Don't go away. I'm sorry."

"As ever," replied the good doctor. And she broke into a trot.

The winners

Jubilation was not a new feeling for Ali, who was used to winning games. But she was never sure if Felicity was feeling what she herself felt. Even now, twenty minutes after a joke game, that last sprint that clinched the match was still alive in her sinews and her mind's eye. But she looked at Flic and saw a woman distracted.

"Good game!" Ali said as her lover messed with the torch.

"Yeah, great... Look at this, you wouldn't think I changed the batteries last month, for God's sake. It's dimming again." She held her hand in front of the torch but to Ali, in the bright light of the tent, it was hard to tell. Still, she did like to see the concentration on her lover's face over these matters of camp survival. Flic took the whole thing very seriously, like a TA captain on exercise. She had once spoken nostalgically of the mini survival kit she made at the age of eight by stuffing various essentials into a fountain pen. Confused, Ali had asked how many essentials would fit into a fountain pen, to which Flic answered that it was a particularly chunky pen bought especially for this purpose, as illustrated in *The Boy's Guide to Living Wild*. That focused expression must have been even cuter back then.

"Flic!"

"Yes, my sweet?"

"Do you think we should pump up the airbed a bit more?"

"What, now? It'll go down again. We should wait till bed-time."

"Sooo, you don't think it's bedtime now then?"

"Hmmm, an interesting hypothesis. You want to test out our new toy, I suppose? You're getting as randy as the new lovers out there." She waved a hand towards the open tent-flap.

"I'm worried about them." Ali was fitting the foot-pump to the rubber mattress. "I can't help thinking we should say something..."

"To whom?"

"Who d'you think?"

Flic rolled her eyes. "Like what?"

"Like, everything we know."

"Don't." She threw down the rubber torch in irritation at either Ali or the torch itself, then collected herself and stretched out her arms to her hi-maint lover. "I don't think that stuff is going to happen any more."

"Based on what evidence, dear?"

Flic rubbed her fleshy nose against Ali's pointy one. "Based on her new maturity? Anyway, we introduced them – we can't go slandering either of them now." She pulled back and cocked her head. "What's that hiss? Have you removed the pump and secured the cap to the... thingy?"

"Don't you know the proper word for the thingy? Call your-self a camper?" As Ali fiddled with the airhole, Bodger came bounding into the tent and leapt delightedly on to the bed. With a whoosh, the air gushed out again. The dog barked.

Flic laughed at her lover's shout of annoyance, then threw herself to the ground. "Darling," she cried, "let *me* be your airbed!"

Her well-padded body did look inviting. To the sounds of barking Bodger and hissing bed, Ali took her up on it.

What the campsite lady saw

There was no one called Dorothy.
   They were definitely That Sort.

3
shift

Silly Putty

Have you seen that Alison Bechdel cartoon where the therapist says that a floundering relationship is like a lump of Silly Putty? Pull it slowly apart and it won't ever break, but wrench it firmly and you have two separate halves, to make new shapes with.

While Drew continued to tell me that I should just settle down with Jennifer and stop agonising and making things worse, others were not so sure. Even my sister Hannah, who had been Jen's biggest fan at the start, had recently said, "Everyone has bad times but you haven't had a good word to say about her for as long as I can remember. Are you sure you want to stay together?"

Sure? Was I sure? I was not sure of anything. Did I want to live in a bedsit, work on a pointless magazine, go out with someone who wouldn't move out of her ex's house? Did I want to be un-happy so much of the time? Was that Jennifer's fault? Could I ever cure myself?

I only ditched the therapist because she was so interfering, not because I didn't want to be helped. What would you say if your therapist told you: "Buy yourself some big thick felt-tip pens and a big roll of paper. You are going to draw whatever you like to express your feelings. You can write in that big thick pen,

'The stupid bitch, she doesn't understand me!'"

She was smiling.

For a second, I thought she meant I should write that about *her*. Then I realised she meant Jennifer. Well, it was certainly true that Jennifer didn't understand me, but how could she? I didn't understand myself. But to call her a stupid bitch?

Was I supposed to react? To say, "Don't you go talkin' 'bout my bitch like that, you ho! You don't call my bitch a bitch!"

Was it a jumping-off point for me to say how I viewed Jen, to modify the therapist's initial suggestion? But I felt tainted, abused, like she thought she'd go inside my head and plant some filth there. And all this had started with a plan for me to "draw whatever I liked", which might actually have been a good idea, given my long-term block around my art. No way could I do it now, with that "bitch" comment banging around in my head.

I fumed all week and eventually rang the therapist and said she was too directional for me and I wasn't coming back. When I looked at everything she had made me do over the years, it was a wonder she'd had any positive impact at all. What was that thing with the piping and the phone book? The yelling? Why did she give me a hug last summer? I didn't ask for it. Was she even qualified? Thank God I didn't go to her group, or that therapeutic retreat in Devon. Jesus. And there was also something seriously wrong with her hair.

So that's why I no longer had a therapist. I did go to the GP but there was a mix-up and we talked about a mole under my arm instead of my mental state.

It's not good to be depressed for a long time. It's not attractive and the weeks and months go by without much definition. If you refuse social engagements, it relieves the interaction problems but it makes life even blander. If you go out, the panics may come on, and not many girlfriends will agree to call a cab at 10pm just as the party's starting to swing, unless they can be shown a physical symptom (asthma and vomiting don't count).

When we went camping at Easter, the fresh air was supposed to do me good, but there were so many people to relate to all the time, it was easier to stay stoned. I know Jen didn't have a very good time. She did not relish the role of Joss-rallier any more than anyone else ever has. (Well, there was that girl who doted on me for the whole of '89 but hey, she had a drink problem.)

Jen said that only I could help me, that she couldn't make me better, but sometimes I thought if she just believed me, it would help. It was as if she thought I could pull up my socks and stiffen my lip and get a new spine and then it would be OK, I would cope with life like she did. Anyone would think I trapped her. But I never claimed to be someone who could cope with life. She saw the way I coped with my neighbour on our very first date. What did she think, I would improve? It hadn't happened. Well, it had happened briefly from time to time – I would wake up full of the joys and they would last for weeks and I would think I was cured – but the blues don't emigrate, they're more like a frog that comes back to the same deep, murky pond when it's time to spawn.

Still, we had some good times and I only had to look at Jen sleeping, or see her smile when I surprised her at work in the park, to remember why we couldn't part.

And we did stuff together. Lots of stuff. We might meet for coffee in the park first thing, if we hadn't spent the previous night together; we might go down to Spitalfields at the weekend and buy a lampshade and some cheese, say, or meet Drew and Clare at the cinema in the week. Sometimes you can get by on automatic, and

Jennifer could probably do that for years if she wasn't hooked up with a manic depressive – or if she never had to go away with me.

It was when she cancelled plans to join me in Manchester for Dad's birthday that my thoughts about All That Was Wrong With The Relationship became obsessive. Apparently her ex – that same jealous ex with whom she still lived – wanted her company because her mother was coming to stay and was a bit of a trial.

Jennifer sent me a letter. (Not an email, certainly not a text message. A good old-fashioned epistle.) I read it on the single bed in the front bedroom of the 1930s semi in which I grew up. I remembered how I'd once fumbled there with a New Romantic. He was a disappointment: we had no sooner put our hands up each other's frilly shirts than he dragged me red-faced into the sun to walk the streets. I'm not sure what I wanted him to do. All they ever really did was put their willies in my mouth and he was too nice to do that. Eventually I told a boyfriend called Jimmy that we were too old to be virgins. Our deflowering was not sexy. Special, yes, but mainly because we'd planned it and we'd followed through and now we were no longer virgins – it all showed an adult sense of purpose, if not desire.

I was thinking all this because I often thought about it when I was back in my old room: how true desire comes late to some people. I never used to look at bodies, I never thought a man had a nice bum or a woman had nice tits. When other people talked like that, I didn't believe they were feeling it in their groins, and I didn't feel it for years. But I felt the other thing. The stirring up in the gut when someone you like sits next to you, smiles at you, makes a joke and laughs. And I never fucking knew that was desire. It makes me angry now, how it was kept from me. Little chances to find out, denied. A school full of bigoted teachers and frightened closets, the adults who wanted to protect me from the dyke I was going to be.

And then God invented Channel 4. Fortunately, I had a telly in my room. (My mum had been trying to sell her car for six months, had reduced the sign in the window to £25, and finally this guy comes up the drive with a portable TV and says, Want to swap?) Minority programming. Women kissing. *Lianna*. Babies from tea-spoons. Pride. And I'm just stock-still in bed with the bristling goosepimples running up and down me like a foretaste of real sex.

That was good, eh? Before I even told myself I was a dyke. When it was just a longing without a name. Before I went to London and started to meet the women I'd seen on those pro-grammes and get them into bed. Before they disappointed me.

Which brings us back to Jennifer. I called her from my mobile. The longer I held the phone pressed to my ear, the greater the aching heat that pounded into my brain. As usual, I could feel the microwaves doing their short-term and/or long-term damage. But I kept it to myself on this occasion because I needed to talk to her urgently and in private.

"Hey!" I greeted her.

"Oh, hi!"

"So, er, got your letter."

"Oh, yeah."

"Look, Jennifer, you don't have to *write* to me just because you've got something difficult to say. You could say it on the phone."

"I was worried how you'd react."

"You don't say." This was not the best line I could have used. There was a long pause in which her breath was so sibilant against my ear that I thought I could feel and understand it. I thought it was her way of trying to gather up her love for me. I tried to feel the same love and express it in kind words, but what came out was: "So when will I see you?"

"Joss, it's you that's gone away, not me."

I lost the battle with the loving thoughts. "Oh, that's right. Away on my own. Why did I do that? Oh, I remember, because I thought you were coming with me!"

"Why are you being like this?"

"Why are you?" I retorted.

"I can't come up there, that's all. It's not such a big deal."

"And yet it was a big enough deal to require a good written excuse." I smoothed out the epistle. "And I quote: 'Melanie really needs me to help with Joan, so I'll stay here for now and see you just as soon as you get back.'" I was deadpan, not trusting myself to do her voice without heavy mockery.

"Yes."

"Why does *her* family come before mine?"

Silence.

I continued: "Jennifer, it seems like you think everyone else needs you, everyone except me."

"Perhaps they do." Her voice dropped and intensified. I recognised this tactic – it was an alternative to shouting, used when her ex was in earshot. "Perhaps everything can't always revolve around you, Joss."

"What?"

"You just expect me to be there for you but there are other people in my life."

I was flabbergasted. "Like your ex and her mother?" Then a new thought occurred to me. "Or is there someone else you need to see, Jennifer?"

"No. What do you mean? There's no one else."

"No one you promised to see as soon as you'd shaken me off?"

"Joss, I'm not even going to have this conversation. Just because I point out some home truths, you accuse me of seeing someone else. When exactly do you think I developed this relationship?"

"Sorry, are you still talking? I thought you weren't even going to *have* this conversation." I pressed NO on the phone for long enough to turn it off completely. My ear ached.

The ache was growing inside me too – the ache that was my constant reminder that I was still alive, the ache that is to the depressive what the heartbeat is to the well-adjusted. I was thus able honestly to tell my parents that I felt unwell and could not accompany them to a concert at the Bridgewater Hall with its beautiful modern architecture. We had taken a good look at its architecture the night it opened, as it happened, and although they had been back many times since, I had not. I would have quite liked another look, but it would have involved listening to classical music all night and there was no way that my soul could stand it. Quite apart from the fact that I don't really like classical music, there would be emotions involved. One is moved when sitting in a concert hall, especially when it is of such fine architecture that it contributes not only to one's appreciation of architecture but to one's appreciation of scale generally, so that, as in a place of worship, the gods come closer. Add to this the sense of civic pride invoked by a magical building in my home city, and the emotion of the music would have surely been too much for me. Panic or crying or a descent into inertia might ensue.

So I stayed in. Hannah wouldn't arrive till the next day and I was alone. I hooked up my laptop to the phone socket in "my" room (now doubling as my parents' study) and went to Dyketown. Oh, Dyketown, the city that never sleeps. Many's the time I've felt forsaken, and many times confused. But it's all right. Etc.

I was still a cybervirgin. I had taken to chatting in the rooms for thirty-something depressed butches and UK-based book-loving lefties and so on. I had not spent long in the rooms called "Pussy Licking by the Pool" or even "Butch/Femme Cyber". And I didn't want to, because I had a girlfriend. Soon after I'd got my computer, in fact, I'd got a girlfriend. Good old Jennifer. With a Jennifer, you didn't need cybersex because you could have the real thing whenever you wanted. Or could you?

That evening, the chatrooms were quiet except for an orgy in Butch/Femme. These orgies were jokey and perhaps not intended as erotic stimulation. Hard to tell, as they seemed to develop spontaneously and involved a lot of "Get over here" till I didn't know who was doing what to whom. Someone called GoGirl invited someone called London Doll to "continue this little chat elsewhere", and I felt a twinge of loneliness.

I didn't want to stick around but I didn't want to log off. I kept the chatroom open while I worked on an email to Clare, and all the while, people were talking dirty and pairing off.

Mail

Clare gave good email. And that's why we continued our correspondence even though there was something not quite right about it.

I hadn't seen much of her since the camping trip where she seduced my best mate. But when she and Drew wanted to ask Jennifer and me to the pictures, it was left to her to email me, and after that we never stopped. We exchanged JPEGs of dubious value. She sent me jokes from the boys at work (she was temping and enjoying attention from both sexes); I sent her anecdotes, nicely honed. I sometimes thought I should be doing all this with Jennifer, not Clare, but then, Jennifer didn't reply to her emails. And neither Clare nor I could do the same with Drew, because Drew was a doctor and didn't have time for this nonsense. Ever since we were students, in fact, she had only had time for nonsense when all the work was done.

Clare, as it turned out, was funnier than I'd realised (though no more grownup). And I was nicer than she'd guessed. So, when I was upset about the shitty phonecall with Jennifer, I mailed Clare. Unless she was round at Drew's, she was hooked up most evenings on a designated phoneline. Surfing and mailing seemed to take up most of her spare time.

From: Joss
To: Clare
Subject: Is my girlf a bitch?

Jenneefer won't come see me :(Does this make her:

a) bitch from hellville

b) person with life of her own = independent = gooood

c) fallen out of love with me and going out with some guy she met up a volcano?

Please advise.

J x

I trawled around for a while, switching between sites that took too long to load and checking in at Usenet, where I had a range of names and had even accidentally replied to my own post on one occasion. By the time I got back to my regular email, Clare was right in there with the following:

From: Clare
To: Joss
Subject: Re: Is my girlf a bitch?

Bitch from hellville. Deffo.

Why won't she fucking come and see you? If you were my girlf, I'd be up there like a shot. In fact, I'd rather be there than here, so if you want me to pretend to be your girlf, I'm right there. Do I have to stay with your parents or can we go to a top hotel?

Let's not tell Drew. It will be our little secret.

Your luvvikins,

xC

From: Joss
To: Clare
Subject: Re: Is my girlf a bitch?

Whoa, slow down, girl. Trust a bottom to ask for a top hotel.
(I assume you are a bottom but if I am wrong, do feel free to
"correct" me.) If I ever seek *you* out in an industrial city of the
north, I will be sure to ask for a bottom hotel. Anyways, haven't
you got a gf of your very own: a handsome doctor with a heart
of gold and a credit card to match? What would you want with
lil ol' me?

From: Clare
To: Joss
Subject: Re: Is my girlf a bitch?

Which reminds me, is *my* girlf a bitch? She is working like all
the fucking time, man. I never get to see her hardly at all. She is
always with a patient if I call. Does she act like this with you?
As for top/bottom, it is really not hard to guess what goes on
between me and Drew, especially as I am sure she tells you it all
during your many special evenings in and out. If she spent as
much time going *in and out* with me, I wouldn't have to look
around for substitutes now, would I?
thinking of u,
xC

From: Joss
To: Clare
Subject: Re: Is my girlf a bitch?

Hey there, make sure to keep flagging up any jokes with little asterisks, it's a big help thanks. You failed to answer one important question: what would you want with me? Moaning about my best friend tells me nothing about the only person I really want to hear about :)

J xx

From: Clare
To: Joss
Subject: You you you

You are just perfect, no more and no less
Question answered?

From: Joss
To: Clare
Subject: me me me

No, the question was not "what's so great about me?" The question was "what would you want with me?"

From: Clare
To: Joss
Subject: You still

What I would want with you is just whatever you would want me to want with you. K?

From: Joss
To: Clare
Subject: Asterisks, use of

This is very handy, isn't it? So if I go like this: *mmm, babe, I like what I'm hearing*, that's a joke, right? We're not using them for emphasis any more, right? Just for joking. So if I go, *you know how to talk to your butch, you slag*, then that is one big fat funny, right? Just thinking aloud here.

From: Clare
To: Joss
Subject: Re: Asterisks, use of

Keep right on thinking aloud. I like it.
xC

From: Joss
To: Clare
Subject: Re: Asterisks, use of

Uh-huh. You like that? There's plenty more where that comes from. But whoops, we may have crossed a line, y'know?

From: Clare
To: Joss
Subject: Re: Asterisks, use of

Whatever. I cross lines every day, babe, so that don't scare me. I gotta go back to the chatroom. Told some illiterate Yank that I'd be there later. You should try it.

Yours except when needed elsewhere,

xC

See what I mean? It was getting inappropriate. Maybe I would be better off with strangers in cyberspace. Clare hung out in Dyketown, but I didn't like it there. It was full of people talking bollocks and then suddenly copping and vanishing while I was asking them about the weather in West Virginia. And didn't Clare have any qualms about how she was supposedly in a monogamous relationship with Drew? She had recently told me that cyber didn't count, wasn't anywhere approaching an affair and – this is where I started to feel queasy about our "sharing" – that she had not told Drew and never would. Just one more little secret.

As I still had the Dyketown window open, however, I watched the two most likely chatrooms for a few minutes to try and catch Clare copping. The rooms were busy, though, and it was hard to tell which was her nickname. Should I have asked her? I was getting excited from the hormones buzzing round cyberspace so I took the name of Buzz and entered the Butch/Femme chatroom with the profile: "What can I do for you, ladies?"

It was seconds before a new window appeared on the screen and the words "Well? What *can* you do for me?" were taunting me.

Now I was in a "private chat", with all the thrilling hope that accompanied it. We exchanged pleasantries, then: "Have you ever put a bottle up your cunt?" asked my interlocutor.

I cocked my head at the screen.

"Have you ever put a glass bottle up your cunt and then broken it inside you?"

I started out by saying, "This is a weird scene, I don't get it," and ended up leaving private, with him (presumably not her) shouting obscenities at me. I told the rest of the chatroom what had happened and they took very little notice until the bastard came back into the room, calling us stuff that I have never heard before, murderously racist and misogynist and anti-lesbian stuff all mixed up together. And it was as if I was hearing it, rather than reading it quoted. He was in our room, coming at us with a broken bottle.

I came offline sweating with fear and adrenaline instead of spent lust. I wasn't safe. My hands were shaking so much that it took minutes to fight through my parents' triple-locked front door into the air. I paced the empty wet streets of my childhood till my heartbeat returned to normal and I had some hope of sleep.

Jennifer didn't even call me next morning, but when I checked my email, Clare was right there.

From: Clare
To: Joss
Subject: Cyber

Feeling any better this a.m.? Why worry about Jen when you're hundreds of miles away? Shouldn't you be out in that famous gay village?
God, did I have a good time last night! I can't believe you haven't got into this cyber shit yet. It's the best sex and you don't have to kick anyone out of bed in the morning. Maybe I should show you around?
xC

So rude

It's hard to write about good cyber because if you're not there, you don't necessarily get it. In fact, if you *are* there, you don't necessarily get it.

So let's say, it's like when you're a kid and you read a book that transports you to the Magic Faraway Tree. And you really go there, you're not pretending.

Or twenty years later, you're on the phone talking to your best mate and her girlfriend's going "Who are you talking to? Who are you talking about?" because she's hearing all these names she doesn't know, and the gossip about them is so thrilling. And the answer is that the two of you are talking about the characters in *ER*, who are like friends to you.

Maybe none of this applies to you. Just insert your own metaphor for Fantasy Land. It's not high-level stuff, is it? And yet... And yet the transportation is such an intense, surprising delight, all over again, each time you catch yourself transported.

So, let's see, it would be round about the time when Jennifer explained her philosophy of sex. Up until then, I was willing to make some compromises to keep the relationship on a workable footing. I know I'm not easy to deal with, I don't always finish the washing-up, my moods are maddening, I'm clingy one day, cut off the next, loving and entertaining on Day Three. But at least I'm predictable in my changeability, you know the good times are a-comin' back; whereas Jen had started out so relaxed and intimate and was now cool and critical. When I asked her about it, she said she was always better at the start of a relationship, full of promise. She fell in love easily and she had fallen for me from the first day in the park. *Why* was not clear – although she used to recite a list of adjectives such as "handsome", "sexy" and "funny".

She only loves someone before she knows them, and cannot sustain her love when she sees the faults, or when the faults persist despite her coaxing and coaching. It's a common problem among dykes. Why else do they break up after two years, just as the other person's patterns shift into focus like a Bridget Riley canvas they've backed away from?

I craved sex as much as ever. Jennifer told me the creamcake analogy: how she likes to eat a creamcake every now and then but could live perfectly well without them.

And I said, "I'm offering you free creamcakes, any time. Isn't that a good thing? Or what? You want the odd custard slice? You want a cherry tart?"

"God, you can make anything sound rude," she replied.

And that talent was to stand me in good stead.

I needed a new nickname, to avoid the twats I'd met as Buzz. I chose CustardSlice and typed in a profile: "London butch ready for fun." I entered the Butch/Femme room.

It was a Monday night, the night when I didn't feel disloyal because Jen was unavailable, staying at home to be teacher's pet in dear Melanie's weekly yoga class, taught in their front room.

I was sitting at my window, looking out at the high street. To counter the incessant background beat of Madam's records, Catatonia were singing quietly on my stereo. Cerys enumerated London's faults as I leapt beyond into cyberspace.

Clare had promised to "meet" me there at 11.30pm, using the handle "LondonDoll". She told me that the word "London" was good bait for those who recognised it, but that some people thought it meant Ontario or even (less understandably) France.

She was there. Lots of people were there. Most of them said hi as I went in – my entrance, like everyone's, having been announced onscreen. Although I couldn't see it, I knew the others had seen the words "Please say hi to CustardSlice: London butch ready for fun."

My compatriate, LondonDoll, continued to talk about the weather with MonicaX, whose profile said only that she lived in Detroit and liked sunsets. I scanned the list of names: Ju-Ju, Claaaarissa, LaydeeLegz, Lippygirl, MADDOG, Butch4U, BootMe, Black_Beauty, Sweet17, IzzyKidd, ZebberD... Their profiles did not reveal much, mostly referring the user to a web address which would take forever to load and would include an unappetising snapshot, religious affiliations, an uninformative job title and a shoe size, as I knew from past visits. Tonight, Clare had promised to guide me through the proceedings by means of "private chats" with her that no one else would know about.

If her climatology with MonicaX was anything to go by, Clare might not prove much of a mentor. But Ju-Ju was now talking to me about London and I gamely expressed delight that she had once visited for three nights and had sung in the karaoke at the

Welly. Yes, she had also been to one bar on Compton; yes, she would be coming back someday.

While we exchanged these mundanities, the room was buzzing with other conversations. Several of the women were discussing what to do when your lover refused to come to a social engagement that she had previously promised to attend. It didn't seem like any hot stuff was going to happen in this room.

I left it up to Clare to work out which was me. The smaller window that eventually popped up on my screen obscured part of the chatroom. It was headed with Clare's nickname and contained her opening gambit: "Hey, Custard! Have you pulled?"

I typed: "Hope not. Where's the action, Dolly?"

"Hmmm, shall we check out Single Cyber?"

"Sounds good. Now?"

But she was already gone. There were 22 people in the room called Single Cyber Fun, having a row about whether one of them was a man. After that person left, muttering to him or herself, feathers were smoothed back down and hellos were granted to the new entrants. Immediately, someone named Yazz asked if I was into heavy action.

"Only with those I know well," I responded, ending with a smiley :) Knowing or twee?

Instead of continuing in this vein, Yazz asked the same question to the room: "Anyone into heavy action?" but was ignored.

I double-clicked on Clare's nickname and the wee private window materialised, in which I typed, "How do you spot the nice ones??"

Her words appeared in response: "Give it time. You know that."

"No, I don't. That's why I'm asking."

"You want slow-burners. They chat for a bit, flirt for a bit, before ACTION."

"& how do u spot the maniacs?"

But I'd lost her attention. I went back to the chatroom to see who she was talking to. She wasn't talking. Given her garrulousness, that probably meant she and someone else were "in private" without any preliminaries. How did she do it? Why did she do it, if slow-burners were best? Even as I thought it, a new window appeared on my screen and LaydeeLegz was introducing herself in rather a crude manner. I went along with it and quickly exchanged a few fantasies but when she asked me to fuck her and I started to talk the talk, a message flashed up: "LaydeeLegz has left private chat or is ignoring you."

I flushed. What? Why? Cow. I checked the main room but her name had disappeared, she had left. So had Clare. Frustrated, I started talking to someone at random by the name of Raspberry, who had just joined. She made a joke. I forget it now, it was inconsequential but it showed she had a sense of humour so I invited her to chat. Safely in private, I asked her why anyone would leave a private chat suddenly in the middle of the action.

"M," she replied.

"???," I enquired.

"Men, babe, you're having cyber with men."

"Ohhh. OK. Every time?"

She was a Dutch fan of Morrissey and The Smiths and wanted to know if I had ever been to the Morrissey Museum. I told her there was no such thing to my knowledge. She directed me to her picture on her own website. She had pasted it on to a picture of Morrissey so it looked almost – but not quite – as if they were standing next to each other. She was wearing a floppy hat and waving an arm like Morrissey might if singing "Will-yuuuum It Was Really Nothing". I was not impressed. It might have looked good or at least interesting on a dancefloor but on a webpage it looked bloody silly. I got rid of her.

The music from Madam's room increased in volume, adding to my irritation. Where was Clare when I needed her? I sent her an email.

From: Joss
To: Clare
Subject: Rubbish chatrooms

Sod this for a game of soldiers. And where are you? You're meant to be initiating me into a wild world of cyberfun with wicked wenches and instead I'm discussing The Smiths' early work with a Dutchgirl (no, no fingers in dykes) while you dally with some slag you've just picked up. What happened to watching and waiting for the ones with wit?
J x

It didn't take her long to reply.

From: Clare
To: Joss
Subject: Re: Rubbish chatrooms

What do you want from me, a free trial session?
xC

From: Joss
To: Clare
Subject: Free trial

With 90 days' approval? But no, I don't want that. I want my own cyberpal, a Notyou cyberpal. No offence but I can't think of many things worse than having cybersex with my best friend's girlfriend. Oh the guilt and self-recrimination. Can't you just fix me up with a nice cyberslut, maybe someone you've finished with?
J x

From: Clare
To: Joss
Subject: Re: Free trial

----

90 days is more than is usually required to fully sample and approve of the service available. Surely the fact that your best mate is fully satisfied with the service should tell you all you need to know. If self-recrimination is all that's stopping you, maybe you should loosen up. The service includes: compliant bottoming and a no-quibbles returns policy.
xC

From: Joss
To: Clare
Subject: Stop that now you naughty naughty girl

Really.

From: Clare
To: Joss
Subject: Ooohhh, say that again

Really.

From: Joss
To: Clare
Subject: Why don't we just use the subject line for the full text of the email and then we would never need to open the mail itself ever again. Not many people realise that there is no limit to how long the subject line can be. Of course there are questions of confidentiality, though, as other people might see the rude bits.

From: Clare
To: Joss
Subject: whatever

I'm going to play with my cyberpals. They don't back off when it gets interesting.
C

Compare and contrast

Jennifer was tall and slim with long, dark curls and neat breasts. She was the same height as me or, on my bad posture days, half an inch taller. When I brushed against her, it was her firmness that excited me, her elasticity, as if I could bounce off her. Clare was small and blonde, blue-eyed, like a cute baby dyke. You might have thought she was 19 instead of 23. She was more rounded than Jen, softer; her gaze was open and teasing and innocent, all at once. How did she do that?

One night, we all went to Popstarz at the Scala. Jennifer was there under duress as she wanted to watch a TV programme about volcanoes but I had persuaded her to tape it instead. She seemed to think she was an expert vulcanologist because she'd been to Lanzarote. Wildlife had long ago taken second place to her new interest in lava. She was not a pleasure to be with in the club but she and Drew got talking in the chillout room about a science topic, leaving Clare and me to dance. We went from floor to floor, on the pretext of looking for Flic and Ali but really because it was more fun than staying in one place. We danced to Pulp, doing our own hand movements to fit the lyrics, then a recent track I couldn't name, then on to the other floor for Abba madness. We were so into it, a double act of wit and skill, weaving around the floor, or so it seemed after six Smirnoff Ices.

The place was heaving with T-shirted boys and girls, smiling and falling over. When we finally took a break, she followed me to the bar. As I yelled my order at the barman, Clare pressed herself into me from behind, her hips thrusting towards my bum so that we moulded together in a moment of warmth. My own hips made a sideways motion, there and back, of their own accord. Almost imperceptible... and an electric charge passed through and between us. That's love. Truly, it felt like love. I shifted to get my money from my pocket. If this move seemed accidental, then she would think I hadn't meant anything a second earlier. Or that I was pretending to have meant nothing. Either way, it was the opposite of turning where I stood and pulling her to me, pressing my mouth to hers... which I did not do. I handed her a bottle of beer and headed back to the floor with my Smirnoff Ice (as clear as your conscience). My cunt was pulsing like a hungry chick. If the cybermaniac had offered to shove the bottle up me at that moment, I think I would have said yes. As it was, I danced and drank myself off my tits.

3am. We moved towards each other. We kissed briefly on the lips. We hugged. Then we kissed on the cheek. Then she got in the cab. I wandered over to the nightbus stop, feeling happy enough, but when I got there I couldn't think why I was alone. Where was my girlfriend? Where was my best friend? Where was the girl I'd been flirting with all night? It wasn't until I was sat on the bus with the side of my face pressed to the cold glass that I realised I was holding a hot pool of tears in my chest. It welled up and out of me with a sentence clear as a voice: "I want them both and I can't have either."

By the time I got home I was trying to convince myself that there are worse things in life than having an attractive woman rub herself against you when you're not available. I tried focusing on a teenage Rwandan woman I'd seen on television who was so positive about the new life she was going to make for herself in this country after fleeing a bloodbath. She used to be rich with a big house and servants; in the UK she didn't get enough vouchers to buy shoes for her little sisters.

I'd been so sad on her behalf that I couldn't even get angry. But now, just a few days later, I was using her as an example of someone worse off than me. She had passed through a door in my head into a symbol of herself. My own family came to this country a hundred years ago to escape the pogroms in Russia and Poland. But they are stories too, because if I feel it for too long, it takes me over, as if it's my own story, and that's not authentic either.

So when Jennifer asked me to go and hear some klezmer in Lauderdale House, in the park, I said no. But every time I turned down one of her suggestions, I was pushing her away. When we finally went out for a meal she said, "You're comparing me with someone else. I can tell. You're looking at me and comparing me to someone. Who is it?"

I shook my head. I looked at the table mat in horror. I didn't want her reading my mind, it wasn't good for either of us.

4
option

A bad reception

In the weeks since the editor's assistant/receptionist had been loudly fired, a succession of temps had managed anything up to six days in the post. But the turnover had not prepared me for seeing one particular new face on the *Modern Interiors* front desk on one particular Monday morning.

"Surprise!" she cried, unnecessarily.

"What the fuck are you doing here?" I asked.

"Working," she smiled.

"Working? Working in *my office*?"

I must have been shouting. The editor, Caroline Chatterby, swung out of her room. "What's going on here?" she asked, her plucked eyebrows shooting up to underline her high, straight fringe.

"Nothing," we both replied.

She looked from one to the other, unable to address us since she was not good with names. Then she swung back into her room. I left the office (which is to say, the large open-plan area across which my shouts had carried to all staff) and took the lift to see my sister, who had recently moved to a new "modern gardens" magazine named *The Outside Room*.

I hadn't yet got used to the journey. In the past it was a case of pushing off from my desk, reverse-wheeling the chair three feet, punting past Tim... and I was at Hannah's desk, ready to tell her about Jen, Clare, Madam, whoever. But now she was way up on the 44th floor and in receipt of my despatches by email or over lunch. I had to change lifts on the way, that's how high up she was.

I was trying to breathe. I knew that not breathing was making it worse, but breathing had earlier led to shouting and I didn't want to shout in the lift. There were people there from one of the countryside magazines, wearing those posh-farmer coats that they consider appropriate office dress. At 44 I got out again. So did they.

In Magazineland, launch titles have a small team based in a small office, either out of the way where no one can see their secret machinations, or next to the mag from which they have spun off. If the launch is successful, the mag gets a proper suite of offices; if it fails in six months (perhaps because the team was so tiny or had not been allocated a colour laser printer) then it doesn't look like a serious failure because there is only one office to shut.

So my sister, in her prestigious new job as chief sub, was sharing a side-room off *Hunting with Dogs* with the entire staff of *The Outside Room*. They were uncomfortable with the topography but it was a sad fact that they had spun off from the whole county/countryside/horses thing and, until they burned their own identity into the reclaimed surfaces of the coffee tables of urbia, their neat black jackets would keep rubbing shoulders with Jaeger on the way to the photocopier.

"Hey, sis!" I greeted her.

She got up to kiss me. "Are you all right?" she asked, scanning my face.

"No. Clare is Caroline Chatterby's new assistant."

"What? Drew's Clare?" She looked as horrified as I was.

"It is a problem, then? It's not my imagination that it's a problem?"

"It could be a problem, if you're still emailing each other in that lewd manner." I bowed my head in shame. "Joss, it's been ages!" I considered the toes of my trainers.

"We danced together..." I mumbled.

"What?"

"Nothing."

She sat me down at her desk and poured me a strong coffee from the office cafetiere. White girls in black clothes were glancing at us over the top of their Macs, to see if sympathy was required or if this was a private sibling moment. Hannah ignored them. "How did this happen?" she asked.

"Well, I cut the ad out of the *Grauniad* and pressed it into her palm as she reached for the popcorn during *Bridget Jones*."

"That's nice of you," said one of the girls, smiling.

I sighed and lowered my voice. "I don't know how it happened. I just went in this morning and she was sat at the reception desk outside Caroline's office. But she could just be temping, right?"

"I heard they'd appointed someone. Someone who hadn't worked in magazines before."

"Doh!"

"Doh. Shall I come back down with you?"

"Come down later and distract me."

I settled at my desk without speaking and tried to do my work. An hour passed, during which I was composing emails to Clare and deleting them.

Hannah came round the corner. "Hi everyone!" she beamed. "Joss, we'll have lunch later, OK?"

"Yeah." Everyone was smiling at her and asking how she was and when the launch issue of *The Outside Room* was due. Geoff, the geeky designer, pointed out that it could be abbreviated to OR, which stands for operating room on *ER*. "Is there blood on the floor?" he asked.

"Come up and see for yourself," said Hannah. "Come in press week. Bring swabs."

"I've got a tube of wet wipes," the art director, Lesley, cried from the other side of the low barrier that emulated a wall without blocking sound or vision and thus was nothing but a psychological prompt – writing "Art Zone" on the floor might have been more useful and less cumbersome. "Take them up with you," she continued. "They'll do for minor scalpel wounds." She brandished the blade she used for slicing transparencies and everyone laughed.

As the *M*A*S*H* atmosphere built up, I was uncomfortably aware that it couldn't be long before Clare was introduced around the office, unless a ward round had already taken place before I arrived that morning.

Scaboosh! Here she was. Chatterbox was leading her towards us, and my sister, being on the wrong ward, scarpered.

"These are the subs," said Chatterbox, waving an arm in our general direction as we smiled back, polite patients.

"Sub-editors," she elucidated. "They check things. They check the spelling and things. They put my spelling right, don't you, subs?"

"Ha-ha, yes," we laughed. In fact we completely rewrote her "Letter from the Editor" every month, except when we were especially cross with her, at which times we left it exactly as she had written it, for all the world to see. Had we switched her photo for a nudey shot, we could not have disgraced her more, but it went right over her well-coiffed head, adding to our satisfaction.

Her eyes stayed on me for long enough to register me as an individual. Then she pointed. "You touch-type, don't you?"

I had helped out by keying in copy when one of the temps stormed off, and Chatterbox had apparently remembered this, though not my name.

"Yes," I replied, raising an eyebrow questioningly. I felt I was making clear that my rank was above that of touch typist, just in case Clare got the wrong idea about my place in the hierarchy.

"So, you two have something in common!" exclaimed Chatterbox. "Because Clare touch-types too! I wish I could, it's so clever!"

Already, people were cooing "Hiiiii Clare" in welcoming, non-threatening tones. A far cry from the *M*A*S*H* reality. As the editor and her new assistant moved on to the next stop on their itinerary, I opened my email to write to Hannah. But she had got there before me.

"Sis: Do you want to ask Clare to have lunch with us? This would prevent you from asking her to dine 'a deux'. Han x"

I replied: "Sis: no fucking way. Let's go out. I'll speak to her tonight. All I can think about is OFFICE AFFAIR, OFFICE AFFAIR. Save me from myself. Thank you."

It was some consolation to be starting a correspondence. It would most likely run all day. In my office, the boss – that is, the chief sub-editor sitting next to me – preferred to communicate by email. Tim seldom turned his head towards me; his laughter was reserved for emails from his friends throughout the building and even beyond the walls of Magazineland. When he appeared to be busy typing, he was writing emails. When he wanted to tell me something of the slightest sensitivity, he emailed me. This meant he never had to say anything difficult out loud. Even if he saw that I was carrying on an email exchange all day long with my sister upstairs, he would not view it as a problem, rather as proof that I was a fun-loving gal with contacts.

It was a while since I had worked anywhere else and I had almost forgotten how a normal office operated. In any case, I liked emailing my sister. I even emailed Jennifer that day, though it was doubtful she would notice.

Perhaps there are more adult ways I could have responded. After all, it was just a friend working in my office, albeit without giving me any advance notice of this new employment. But I was so excited that I couldn't even think about it, let alone find an adult response. I guess it was the middle of one of my manic episodes – I hadn't been right for days. These episodes are hard to describe to other people, especially the sceptics. The homeopath has suggested that we think more in terms of mood swings, or at least use the language of mood swings when talking to other people, but I find that the sentence "I have quite bad mood swings" evokes no response whereas "I have mild manic depression" is pretty much guaranteed to generate an argument that will bring me close to tears and so prove my point.

Circumstances don't tend to dictate the mood. Sometimes I think it's the other way round. Do I ever get lost, for instance, when I'm *not* having a mixed episode? What follows is that I get off the bus (if I'm on a bus at the time of getting lost) without asking anyone where I am, and sob as if something so shocking and damaging has happened to me that I am on the verge of collapse. I am ignored for long enough to remember to breathe, to start breathing, to feel myself as a channel of energy between the sky and the earth... All that stuff. And eventually I call someone on my mobile to say I'm lost and scared, or I get back on the same numbered bus *and no other* on the opposite side of the road and go home.

Well, finding Clare on reception was not like getting lost. It was more of an up moment because of the excitement and because it so happened that I was already hyper, already manic. But that's when I know it's not long before the crash comes.

I want to be correct about this. I want to detail the difference between depressed and manic, between one or other of them and the dangerous *mixed state* (a state which I imagine doctors had to invent when they realised that some patients wouldn't stay as one thing or the other for long enough), but I can't get there. I want to keep a diary of my moods, but I can't stay there.

For now, I'll just say that the day when Clare started work at *Modern Interiors* was a day when I glimpsed the forthcoming crash and tucked it back behind my blind spot so it could catch me unawares later instead of scaring me ahead of time.

Twilight zone

That evening, I was itching to phone Clare. But while I dithered, she called.

"Hi babe!" she said cheerfully.

"Oh, hi. How are you?" *How are you?* Will my habits never change? Will that be the first thing I say when they phone to tell me the results of the biopsy?

"I'm fine," she chirruped. "I've got a new job!"

"Funnily enough, I noticed."

"Don't you think it's cool? I'm in your office!"

"Clare, have you gone mad? Why didn't you tell me you were applying?"

"Oh, I didn't realise at first that it was your magazine. And when I did, I'd already had the interview."

"Right. You must have been well prepared for it, then."

"It doesn't always matter in my line of business. They just want to know if you can type and use initiative and all that."

"And when they hired you, you forgot to mention it to me?"

"It was only on Friday."

"Friday! I saw you on Friday night in Due South!"

"I know. I wasn't sure if I was going to take the job and I didn't want you to influence me."

"Clare, don't lie to me."

"What?"

"You must have accepted it on Friday, if you started today. You kept it from me, so you could see my face this morning. Well, I hope you enjoyed it." I put the phone down. Then I was disappointed that there wouldn't be a row. Why had I done that?

I rolled a joint and turned on the TV. It was the very latest in reality gameshowing and I had just begun a lively debate with myself about the meaning of entertainment when the phone rang again.

"What?" I asked rudely.

"Nice to hear your voice too, darling." Jennifer.

"Oh hi, sorry, I thought you were Clare... I just hung up on her."

"Aha. The Joss School of Friendship. What happened?"

"Fuck, Jen, you won't believe this. She's working at *Modern Interiors*."

"Oh, that."

"What do you mean? You knew?"

"Yeah, she told us in Due South on Friday, when you were in the loo. She wanted to surprise you so I promised not to tell you. I thought you'd be pleased."

Since Jen had no idea that Clare and I were embroiled in a near-adulterous flirtation, I could hardly explain how the little minx had made glove-puppets of us all with her "surprise".

"Well, I'm *not* pleased," I said instead. "And I can't believe you would deceive me like that. All of you. Jesus. I thought I could trust *you*, at least." It did not escape me that this was a tad unjust in the circumstances.

"God, Joss, what's the matter? Aren't you pleased she's working with you?"

"No, I'm not, as it happens. I like to keep my work life separate from my personal life."

"You work with your sister."

"I don't. I mean, I did, but now she's thirty floors above me and I only see her at lunchtime. Anyway, it's not the same. How would you like it if Drew started working in the park?"

"What, prescribing antibiotics to the rescued hedgehogs? I'd love it. She'd have something more to talk about than *Animal Hospital*, unlike my colleagues."

"I wouldn't count on it. If you pick up her copy of the TV guide next time we're there, you'll notice she's circled everything that might include medical opinion. Anyway, the point is that you should not have lied to me."

"I didn't. I just kept a secret for a friend. Why do you have to make such a big deal out of everything?"

"This is not everything. This is my friend starting work in my office without telling me. Don't you think that is a little weird?" I was exhausted and she must have noticed, as her voice became more sympathetic.

"Yeah, you're right actually." She took a fair stab at the internationally recognised sound for Twilight Zone. "It seemed normal on Friday after three pints and a tequila slammer but now it does seem a bit odd. What's she up to?"

"Just enjoying the power games, that's all. That's what she does."

"You never said that before. What else has she done?"

"Oh, nothing specific. But if you think about how she seduced Drew on the camping trip –"

"That doesn't count. You might as well say you were playing games with me when we first met in the park."

Indeed. "As you wish."

"And come to think of it, the main reason Clare got asked to come camping was because Drew fancied her from that party. So that's not Clare's fault, is it? It was Drew who was sneaky."

This was not making me feel any better. So we were all as underhand as each other. Great. I could hear Jen running the tap and then lighting the gas.

"Am I keeping you?" I asked with mild sarcasm.

"I'm starving, actually. I'll speak to you later, OK?"

"OK," I said sulkily.

"Bye then."

"Bye." I put down the phone and roared with repressed anger and disappointment. Why wouldn't she sympathise? The tears started just as the phone rang again. Unable to protect myself, I picked it up. It was the digitalised BT lady to tell me I had a new message on Call Minder. That was Clare, of course, chirpy and apologetic.

Fuck her.

Next time the phone rang, it was Ali calling from Eastbourne. Apparently Navratilova had made some errors in the doubles. Ali never misses the tournament but as she is a teacher, she has to make up a different excuse each year for her time off. Last year she had a road accident of some severity and this year her poor mother is on her last legs in Hastings.

I wasn't sure why she had called. "Why have you called?" I asked.

"Oh, *pardonnez-moi!*"

"I only mean that you never call me."

"Well, now that I'm away, I've had some time to think about Drew and Clare. I'm a bit worried about them and I wanted to talk to you."

Ha! "What do you mean?"

"I just don't know if Clare is up to it. Drew is so involved with her, but do you think Clare is?"

"Clare is what?"

"Involved. And… loyal."

"Ali, is this some kind of trick?"

"What?"

"Is Clare there with you or something?"

"No. Of course not. She hates tennis. What are you talking about? I just can't ever talk about this when I'm in London. Flic won't let me discuss it with anyone."

"So you're calling *me* now. You've never called me before in your life."

"I have! I invited you to Flic's birthday!"

"Last *November*!"

"Oh for God's sake, Joss, talk to me."

"OK, you can have five minutes."

What she told me was far from reassuring. I went for a walk afterwards. It was the longest day of the year and the park was still sunny, but only a few people were strolling around it or feeding chocolate mousse to each other on travel blankets, that kind of thing. I could see the millennium wheel through the trees, miles away.

I climbed back up the slope past the bird sanctuary and the gate to Jen's lodge and then the statue of Sir Sydney Waterlow who gave this park as a garden for the gardenless. In three more minutes I would be on the high street and would have to choose which grocer's to visit for my tea. But first I had to brave a small group of pre-teen white boys slouching in the grass.

"I don't like lesbians," one of them called as I passed, projecting clearly in BBC English.

"Well I don't like little boys, so we're quits," I replied.

"But lesbians are worse," he parried.

"I think not," I managed, on my way through the gates to freedom, to the rules of the street, which are not quite the same in Highgate as elsewhere. In Highgate, no one would be so rude as to declare they don't like lesbians to a lesbian on the street.

I went to the further grocer and noticed that some older white boys were scattering round the shop as if in preparation for a little shoplifting. I bought a Patak's frozen curry and a quarter-pound bag of Bird's Eye peas as I pondered whether that particular boy would have called "I don't like black people" after a black person. I concluded no.

Why do they hate me? Why do they hate me? I chorused in my head as I paid the Middle Eastern grocer. I don't usually think of him as a Middle Eastern grocer but difference and diversity were uppermost in my mind and white boys were low down the hierarchy.

When I got back to the flat, I put the containers in the microwave and the peas on the stove, and the phone rang.

"Hi, how are you?" said Drew.

"OK, how are you?"

"Look, are you all right with Clare at your work?"

"Why wouldn't I be?"

"And what's going on with Ali?"

"What do you mean?"

"She's acting weird. If you knew something, would you tell me?"

"Something about what?" I chewed nervously on a frozen pea.

"Are you eating?"

"Are we playing that game where you have to answer every question with a question?"

"I don't know, are we?"

I ate my tea pondering why I had not had a normal conversation all day. Was it something I was doing wrong? Was it the solstice? Was it just my perception? I logged on to the net.

Private chat

In Dyketown, girls from around the world come together. Most of them are in the English-speaking world, most of them can type fast. Let's face it, most of them are American. Did the American school system know when it taught its kids to type that this would one day be the skill that helped them to keep right on running the world?

Amy is in America. Amy has met someone she likes in a chatroom in Dyketown and they have flirted there until agreeing to a private chat. Though Amy is a way upfront kinda gal, she doesn't rush into private. She waits to be wooed there, waits till the pull is irresistible and they both know it's going to be fun. That just happened.

<amy~> hey you!
<CustardSlice> Hey, Noo York girl. How come you get to live in my dreamtown?
<amy~> u been here?
<CustardSlice> Nah! But I want to!
<amy~> so hop on an airplane, girl.
<CustardSlice> Is that an invitation?

<amy~> sure, i like english girls
<CustardSlice> Oh, all English girls? Nothing personal then?
<amy~> how personal do u want?
<CustardSlice> Weeeell... how personal do u get?
<amy~> for the right girl, *very* personal
<CustardSlice> Oh, look, your Prez just came on TV!

Whaaaat? Amy wants to hear "Mmmm" or "Let me tell you about the right girl right now" or "Get over here and say that". Amy wants progress, she wants innuendo that sticks. She keeps on keeping on but it seems Custard has many ways of staving off the feature presentation, not least her irritating references to what she's watching on TV. Time for Amy to take charge.

<amy~> how you feeling tonight, babe?
<CustardSlice> Hmmm, horny.
<amy~> yeah? cool. what do u like?
<CustardSlice> Look, I have to say I am having like zero luck with this whole cyber thing. People keep fucking off in the middle.
<amy~> guys
<CustardSlice> So I'm told.
<amy~> don't believe it??
<CustardSlice> I guess anyone who says they've got massive bazooms and a silky nightie and long curly blonde hair is on a weird trip, huh?
<amy~> but that perfectly describes me!
<CustardSlice> ???
<amy~> LMAO!
<CustardSlice> ???
<amy~> it's a joke babes

<CustardSlice> OK, I knew that. (phew)

<amy~> soooo, what do u look like??

<CustardSlice> Tall, dark, going grey, big brown eyes, "medium build", as they say. Combats and Ts. I pull a lot of faces.

<amy~> cute and honest

<CustardSlice> What's not to be honest about?

<amy~> like you say, kinda unusual. what else?

<CustardSlice> People take me for butch

<amy~> but?

<CustardSlice> But nothing. Tell me about yoooo.

<amy~> i am 26, black, kinda dark-skinned, 155cm, long locks, pierced eyebrow, cute but not massive bazooooms :)

<CustardSlice> Nice

<amy~> and while we're there, pierced nipples toooo ;)

<CustardSlice> Verrrry nice

<amy~> i like butch women but i'm not exactly femme...

<CustardSlice> Uh-huh. Wearing?

<amy~> just a robe

<CustardSlice> Perfecto.

<amy~> have u got a girlfriend?

<CustardSlice> Yeah. U?

<amy~> no but i'm not looking

<CustardSlice> So why do u ask??

<amy~> just wondering what kind of girls you're into

<CustardSlice> Gorgeous ones like u babe :)

<amy~> :)

<CustardSlice> Soooo, this is going well...

<amy~> and therefore?

<CustardSlice> And therefore it could perhaps go a little further.

<amy~> mmmm. what ru into?

They got there, they reached the beginning of the ritual.

If the two parties are a good match, their fantasies will meld from the start: each will say what the other wants to hear, picking up clues so small that they seem not to have been typed at all, but plucked from the ether or transmitted by a telepathy that links minds instead of bodies, better than bodies, as well as bodies; that links minds and cyberbodies down the line.

Custard and Amy have that match. They amaze themselves and each other as the map of their potential lovemaking unfurls on-screen and segues into the act itself. Amy sits at her desk, playing with her hair, then her tits, then pushing her left hand inside her robe as she types with the right. And Custard lies back on the bed with her laptop and tells Amy to stop typing. Custard grinds her hips into the bed as she types as fast as she has ever typed, giving Amy the words she needs to get off.

It's just as well that the screen scrolls quickly up and the words are lost, because that's not where the poetry is. The fucktalk works because the chat worked, because they laughed together and heard each other's laugh. And as a result, when they come, it's like the climax of a hot date that lasted all night. And then they rest.

<CustardSlice> Want a spliff?
<amy~> a what?
<CustardSlice> Joint
<amy~> yeah!
<CustardSlice> Rollin
<amy~> you are hot
<CustardSlice> Uh huh and so ru
<amy~> nice
<CustardSlice> Uh huh. Here, talk to me while I roll.

<amy~> weeeell...

<CustardSlice> Talk!

<amy~> resting!

[pause]

<CustardSlice> K. Here's the splifferooni 4 u.

<amy~> toking. nice

<CustardSlice> U really called amy?

<amy~> yeah

<CustardSlice> So what's with ~ ?

<amy~> so my friends know it's me i guess

<CustardSlice> Funnily enough, this is not my name.

<amy~> what is it?

<CustardSlice> Not telling

<amy~> but what is custard slice?

<CustardSlice> Squelchy English delicacy.

<amy~> yum

<CustardSlice> u can lick out the middle

<amy~> double yum <flashing tongue @ u>

<CustardSlice> :)

<amy~> ever use your real name?

<CustardSlice> Nah

<amy~> because?

<CustardSlice> Dunno. Saving it.

<amy~> for what?

<CustardSlice> Dunno!

<amy~> u r gonna tell me it??

<CustardSlice> Er no

<amy~> and i thought we were close :)

<CustardSlice> So did I!

[pause]

<CustardSlice> ... And I'd love to see u again. Cutegirl.

<amy~> uh-huh me too

<CustardSlice> Gooood

<amy~> goooooood

<CustardSlice> :)

<amy~> ;)

[pause]

<CustardSlice> Y'know it's 3am here, I gotta sleep babe. You are soooo good.

<amy~> go to sleep babe! good to meet ya :)

<CustardSlice> Ditto   :)

<amy~> sweet dreams sweet girl

<CustardSlice> Yeah, you too hon.

amy~ has left private chat or is ignoring you

Amy doesn't like to play mindgames, but there is one little matter on which she agrees with the authors of *The Rules*: always be the first to hang up (or close that window). Hey, Custard has her email address, there in London, England, where it is late at night. Amy has a smile on her face as she lets her head loll back to gaze at the ceiling. Something tells her that butch won't go to sleep without mailing her.

Madame's appartement

"Joss! Come and see my room!" Madam's excited smile made me tense with anxiety.

Anxiety about forthcoming events and anxiety about events in the past are two separate categories in a homeopath's book. The patient will be asked – and I had often been asked – "Are you worrying about things that have happened or things that might happen?" I usually answered "Both."

By now, I was using my homeopath for all-purpose therapy, truly holistic. She had never encouraged me to discard the psychotherapist, the yoga classes or the osteopathy. On the contrary, she still made comments such as "I'm not a counsellor" or "That sounds like a problem with posture" which I chose to ignore but which were surely meant to lead me to seek help elsewhere.

Once, when I listed all my mood symptoms in one go, she opened a *Materia Medica* and, unprecedentedly, handed it to me. "Read 'Mind'," she urged. The page was Cannabis. The reported symptoms listed under "Mind" included: excessive loquacity, exuberance of spirits, moaning and crying, constantly theorising, fixed ideas, extreme psychic mobility, when he speaks it seems as though someone else is speaking, sensation of flying, fear of insanity, ridiculous speculative ideas.

My eyes widened as I read. How had I failed to notice that the effects of cannabis were so similar to my mood symptoms? Why was I treating my illness with a drug that caused the same effects, in an unconscious parody of homeopathy?

"It builds up in the system," she told me.

"I'll stop smoking then," said I.

"Really?" she asked, surprised.

"Of course. Why wouldn't I?"

I quit for a month but recommenced after a casual comment from Jennifer to the effect that I was worse than ever. I told this to the homeopath who said it takes six weeks to leave the system. Like so many things in life, I hadn't really given it a chance.

I mention this now because much of my anxiety in Madam's presence could probably have been attributed to the effects of cannabis. When she was at her worst, three years back, I used to have all those "speculative ideas" that she was dead in the bath or being attacked by her boyfriend, and I was usually stoned when I had them. Still, I wasn't stoned that time when she was so ill she called me into her room and flapped her skinny arm above the covers – that was for real, it was the last time I'd been in there, and it didn't make me want to go back.

Now I followed her through the open door. The floor was still poorly painted in white emulsion but a beige rug covered the worst of it. The bed was in one piece and draped in an orange flowered duvet cover; the curtains, old and nasty as ever, hung at the window in preference to the bed. It was a normal room.

"I've been thinking," she began excitedly, her eyes never leaving mine (which meant I had to keep up a neutral/interested expression without a flicker of fear or evasion), "that this room needs a makeover. I haven't got any money and *Changing Rooms* never wrote back – maybe we should have written in together – but your magazine could do it."

"Oh, I don't know." And I didn't know. The first rule of magazine makeovers is "Never use the public". But there are only so many staff and true friends who want their houses vamped and re-vamped and many say "Never again" after the first time.

The magazine had moved downmarket in the last few months. The publishing director, Lavinia Buff-Jones, had taken a special interest in it and, armed with a list of the country's best-selling titles on which *Modern Interiors* languished too low, she concluded that it would do better if it copied a rag named *102 Lovely Houses and Flats.*

This seemed to show a basic misunderstanding of the purpose of *Modern Interiors* – to fill a gap in the market as a glossy for people renting flats in London but longing for a loft in Manhattan. They might not be the broadest band of consumers but they were easy to target and as aspirational as they come.

However, Ms Buff-Jones had other ideas. I had never seen her, but rumours about her management style suggested she would not feel the need to consult the editor on the changes. As it happened, Chatterbox did not object to lowering her brow: the target reader-ship was one she knew and adored from her time as deputy editor of *Your Gorgeous Home*.

The planned mix for the all-new *Modern Interiors* was lots of beautiful rooms and a good splash of TV stars (we used the term loosely). A distinction that might more wisely have remained in the editorial meeting was allowed to seep on to the pages of the magazine: the distinction between a Real Reader and a friend or relative of the staff *portrayed* as a reader. In the future, not only would readers be encouraged to send in photos of their lovely houses and flats, but these photos would actually stand a chance of featuring in the magazine, under the strapline "Real Reader's Home" – a clue to the bright-eyed that some Readers were less real than others.

So what was Madam?

Certainly not a Real Reader – aside from devouring the magazine, they also sent in letters and dark snapshots of their stencilling handiwork, from satellite towns, new towns, garden suburbs and Essex. And those who had failed to notice that they were no longer our target readership continued to send shots of the customised island units in their Pimlico kitchens.

A Friend or Relative, on the other hand, was someone who might not have approached us at all, but might have *been* approached, to have their homes photographed with or without a part-paid makeover. They fell into four categories:

1. Friend or relative who likes nice things and lovely homes but can't quite afford them.

2. Friend or relative who has nice things and lovely home and wants to show them off in mag.

3. Work contact who wants free editorial in guise of feature about own house (e.g. curtain-maker, cushion-coverer, finial-turner).

4. Member of staff on the make, often doing deal with provider of carpet/furniture/decking.

We had been warned not to use friends who wouldn't understand if it took forever or if it went over budget and they had to mop up the excess themselves. Madam would be crap on both fronts. Nor was she a friend. So she didn't fall neatly into Category 1. And she sure wasn't Cat 2 – we were not looking at a lovely home, here, but a lowly bedsit that she didn't even own.

However, a memo had been circulated only last week, urging all staff to join the search for hundreds of rooms, flats and houses to be photographed and/or improved. A bedroom supplement was forthcoming. Could Madam's room be part of this?

I told her to leave it with me. But Jennifer's advice later that day was to check with Dr Drew whether she thought Madam (who was still under her care) was up to it.

Drew, it turned out, wasn't telling. "First, she does have a name apart from Madam," she chastised me. "Second, I can't discuss a patient. I've told you before. Speak to her yourself, don't ask me about your own bloody neighbour."

"Oh, bloody now? So she annoys you too? So you see her as a problem?"

"I didn't say that, and I'm not saying anything. Shall I book for Catatonia at the Forum?"

"Oh, interesting segue. Naming a neurological disorder in the same breath as Madam."

She groaned. "I'm booking for me and Clare tomorrow. Let me know."

Yeah right. An outing with my asexual lover, my best friend and her clit-tease of a girlfriend to see a sex goddess was just what I needed right then.

"You know what?" I said. "Don't bother. Cerys will have a breakdown, the tour will be cancelled, and you'll have to get your money back. Don't we learn anything from past experience?"

"I don't know, mate, do we?"

Most improved new small profit centre

I opened the first of three emails from my boss, who was sitting next to me as usual. The first, headed "Dalai Lama", purported to be an urgent spiritual message to the universe which needed to be passed on quickly if the recipient was to avoid bad luck. Tim had added to it: "Don't usually pass these on but hey man, my karma means a lot to me and what if it's for real?" He had sent it to 27 people.

I replied tersely before opening his second missive, headed "Whoops", with its mini-movie of a man in a zoo whose head suddenly disappeared up an elephant's bum. I watched it twice and was unable to discern whether or not it was an optical illusion.

The third email was more useful. Headed "Most improved new small profit centre award", it was a message he had forwarded from Lavinia Buff-Jones who was apparently an authority on the criteria for the annual Magazineland awards, nicknamed the Maggies. I knew that Tim had procured this for me because of my interest in whether my sister's launch mag might qualify.

The criteria read as follows: "A new profit centre is less than two years old. A small profit centre is one with fewer than 12 staff. An improved profit centre is one which has made a dramatic and sustainable improvement in the course of the year, from failing to succeeding or from low profit to high profit."

The Outside Room thus appeared to qualify on all fronts. I forwarded the message to my sister, urging her to check that the editor had nominated them.

Then I should have started some work work, but I was like a moth to a headtorch with the Madam makeover idea. What would happen when a woman with an irony bypass had her home made over by one of the *Modern Interiors* madmen? Would they try to get her to pick up some funky retro pieces in the cancer shop, from which she had been banned for years? Would she insist that the whole room had to be pink to match her new skirt? Was I being totally unfair, given that she had been within gobbing distance of mental stability for some time, which was more than could be said for me? And so on.

I ran the idea by Tim in an email and he loved it. He had always maintained that the magazine should be entirely filled with features chosen by the subs.

"Just to confirm: this is my nutty neighbour," I wrote.

"Just to confirm: all the more fun for Sir Lancelot," he replied, with a reference to our least favourite makeover maestro.

Next I would need to talk to the features editor, a scary woman named Kitty. It could wait. I settled down to subbing a piece called "Me and My Understairs Cupboard", a regular column featuring a different D-list celeb each month.

There were three reasons why I liked subbing this piece. One was that my interest in home decor had declined over the years (having peaked for a matter of months around the time I moved in to my bedsit), and therefore anything that wasn't really about decorating seemed more interesting than anything that was.

Secondly, "Cupboard" could usually be relied upon to have a connection with television, and as television was my main hobby, that was another plus. But the third reason was that the regular columns provided the mag with some identity, much needed since the move downmarket "to gain a wider readership" had resulted in it losing its voice as badly as a rookie teacher in an inner-city comprehensive.

Today I was delighted to see that the interviewee was a minor TV host. His latest venture was a gameshow in which contestants from all over the continent must convert sums of money into euros and back very quickly while the other team shouted non-obscene abuse at them in five languages. Trixie in Features had written the piece herself and some professional instinct told me she might not have read it through before filing it.

Underrstairs

"This cubpoard is not big enough for the both of us! I keep putting stuff in here but Kelly takes it out again, the anugjty girl! I tell you waht though it's better than the loft! Heaven only knows how to get in the loft- and I should know because we've been trying for long enough! We've lived here for two years' now! Anywya, the animals certainly liike it under here and once we found the cat Rolf eating the fertiliser! Fortunately we have a friend who is a presenter on a well known animla hostpial programme and they could help by telling us that the cat would be alright soon. That is probably be the funniest thing that has happned in our understair cupboard but in this house anything is possible!"

Box: Steal the look!
To copy Chirs and Kellys stylish cupboard, line the door with
adhesive fab ric annd paint the interior to match.

Captions: 1. "This cupboard is not big enough for the both of
us" (Chirs in cupboard with hoover)
2. "Mangez moi!")Box of fertiliser)
3. "We need more space!" (Chris with dog)
4. "You naughty boy!" (Kelly wags finger at Chirs)

Improtant Note to subs: Do not phone the couple becausee of
divroce pending.

I took a look at the transparencies, holding them up to the
light. They did not appear to match the piece. In one, the celebrity
couple were sitting in the understairs cupboard in humorous
cramped postures, frowning theatrically. In another, "Chirs" was
feeding the cat from a bag of fertiliser – possibly Caption 2. But
most of the rest were shots of red cushions.

Now I had one more reason to enter the lioness's den of the
features department. I glanced across. Kitty was frowning at her
underling, Trixie, who was using her horsey telephone voice to get
free decking for her father's country estate, showing a sophisti-
cated understanding of the Makeover Cat 2/Cat 4 composite. I
could hear her promising to credit the decking company in the
April issue of *Modern Interiors* – just the kind of promise that did
not go down well with Kitty. But the pair were not speaking (had
not spoken across seven years and three magazines, Trixie
doggedly following her leader wherever she went), so Kitty's dis-
pleasure would be expressed non-verbally within the department

– and highly verbally outside it, to anyone who would listen.

If I positioned myself as Kitty's bile bin, then, I would have her attention. I rang her extension.

"Sorry to bother you, Kitty, but I wonder if you could come over and look at some pix?"

"Who is this?"

"It's me, Joss, the sub."

"Oh, hello, dear. What is it?"

"I wonder if you could come over and look at some pix?"

"Where are you, dear?"

"Er, at the subs' desk."

"Yes, yes." She put the phone down without looking at me. Would she come over? She remained seated for some minutes but then rose with fresh purpose and bustled across to me.

"Yes, dear?" she asked, leaning over me, breathing heavily.

"Are you all right?" I asked.

"No," she whispered hoarsely, "I'm furious! That little... Trixie has promised an editorial credit again. And for her father's garden!"

"Really? God, that's bad."

Easy as that. I listened for ten minutes, she gave me the right pix for the understairs cupboard, I told her about my neighbour's bedsit and she said it sounded perfect for a piece on helping your son or daughter improve their nasty student digs.

Sorted.

Private chat 2

After a post-date mail that made her smile, Amy knew Custard wasn't going to wait long to set up another date. Amy has more than one cyberbutch on the go at once and she tries not to get hung up on any one of them because they tend to have girlfriends in the meatworld. But Custard, with her near-newbie naivety, will not yet have collected a cyberharem or flipped into guilt about the gf. She will be focused on Amy.

And sure enough her next email reads simply: "Midnight Monday, my time, Butch/Femme. Don't keep me waiting, cutegirl. The Slice x"

It exhibits a certain swagger that is attractive but Amy would usually opt for more intelligence, less swagger, and at least one truly personal touch, at this early stage.

"You wanted the talk, you got the talk, you still not happy, girl-friend?" she chides herself as she writes the letter C on her wallchart for Monday, the same day that she hopes to finish the long paper on synergy she has worked on for two weeks. She will deserve a little reward.

What the makeover maestro sees

The address certainly fooled him. When they said a Highgate studio, he anticipated something a little more bohemian. And the girl is not quite the class he expected there either – and such a chatterer, he thinks at first they'll be there all day. In fact, the recce doesn't take long, just the one poky room, and Camilla does a quick measure while he lets some colours come to him. Pink seems too obvious and yet... It suits the girl, it suits the space, it suits the season – spring, hard to imagine but it will come eventually, it does most years.

The magazine said "think student digs" but she doesn't have any books, which is the obvious way to say "student". So he's thinking, either that wallpaper that's all book covers (but Kitty said he must avoid anything that a landlord might veto, which is *rather* limiting), or they do the pink thing (Oh, hark at him, he can't let go of it!) and sod the student thing... Or they have a little desk for her that folds away – that might work, something on hinges.

Poor bloody girl seems to have no life to speak of. Keeps drivelling on about her neighbours like an old biddy. He's thinking, this is his bit for the community, frankly. He must have a word with Kitty: the places they're sending him are getting worse and worse. He can work miracles, yes, but it costs, and he doesn't hear their budgets getting any bigger. It wasn't like this in the old days. Oh no, *Modern Interiors* was a force to be reckoned with then. He remembers going to Astrid Merlin's pad and her saying, "I can't believe I finally made it into *MI*. Do whatever you like, Lance darling, I can't wait!" And what does he get now? "'Ere, are you the guy from that magazine? It is for free, innit?"

Dulux Colour Palette 80YR68/100, the retro circles duvet from BHS... He'll get there.

Yes, she is a lesbian

February was a time when people got upset about how long they'd worked for the company. If you had seen more than two awards ceremonies then it was generally accepted that you had stuck around too long and had better take a look at Monday's *Guardian*. At *Modern Interiors*, that covered most of us. And then there was the annual debate about What To Wear.

The more radical men and the ungroomed made plans to wear a business suit. "I'm not spending money on clothes!" they could be heard to cry. "For God's sake, it's not like I don't have a suit already, who needs a fucking DJ?"

The girls and women, meanwhile, needed new frocks and they needed them now. Whenever anyone asked what I was going to wear, I said I didn't know. And it was true. In past years I had tried different combinations but I had not been happy in any of them. So, was I going to buy a dinner suit, as if I was a man? Was I going to wear my funeral suit, as if I was a man who didn't have a dinner suit? Was I going to borrow a skirt? (No.) Or was there some fourth way, like an ethnic wrap that had not even been invented yet, which would render me so elegant that the gender/formalwear necessity melted away?

The clothing dilemma was a microcosm of my wider discomfort. I fitted in fairly well on *Modern Interiors*, which attracted misfits. There was little compulsion towards conformity and people told each other things they might more wisely have kept to themselves. They liked me being lesbo, because it was cool, maybe even glamorous. But what they didn't know was the crying thing, the aching heart thing, the hole in my aura above my left breast that opened up and let everyone else's bad vibes straight in. The hole that hurt if you touched it. They didn't know any of that.

And when it came to the company as a whole, to the straight straight men and women who got in and out of the lifts in Magazineland, well, I didn't feel at home. True, there were a couple of dozen folk working on the music mags and the cycling titles who all had a note of alternativeness about them, but they weren't really a threat to the status quo. The muzos looked at themselves in the mirror to check the logos were showing on their clothes; while the cyclists talked about expensive gizmos in tones that suggested they were just as susceptible to the label culture.

Whereas I looked like a girl who had forgot she was a girl, or a guy who was a poof.

Maybe it was the delusions of grandeur that accompanied the manic episodes, but I was frequently convinced that people were looking at me whenever I left our office to drop the twenty floors to the coffee shop. Jennifer had noticed it from the start – in the park at our first meeting, in fact, she saw members of the public staring at me in a near-hostile fashion. She was always keen to point it out on the tube. "They're looking, they're looking. Yes, she is a lesbian!" she would shout, under her breath. Partly, she was enjoying the age-old transformation: the femme becomes a recognisable lesbian only when on the arm of her butch. Partly she wanted me to be noticed, wanted me to be special. She even took it upon herself to discuss with my friends what a deeply unhappy person I was under the sociable veneer. Just to make sure there was no one left who thought I was OK, who thought I fitted in.

But now, she was coming shopping to find me something suitable to wear to the Maggies.

Joss sticks

Perhaps it was foolish of us to think we could just "pick up something a bit unusual in Covent Garden". The phrase acquired a certain irony as the day wore on.

"Look at you. A smoothie in one hand and a mobile phone in the other. The essence of Londoner," said Jennifer as we sat in a juice bar in Neal's Yard slurping our Revitalisers and enjoying a rare day of bonding.

"Fook off. I'm not from down here, right?" I grinned at her. "Anyway, look at you with your Angel Cards. What did they cost you?"

"You can't put a price on insight, my dear." She tapped the tiny pack of cards, the size and shape of a wine-bar box of matches. "Pick a card, any card."

I took them out, shuffled them and pulled one from the middle. "Ha!" I cried as I handed it to her.

"'Joy'! Who she?"

I smiled. "Just a blast from the past."

She picked one for herself and considered it.

"What is it?"

"Guess."

"Tell me."

She slipped the card into her back pocket. "It spoils it if you share it."

"What is it then? 'Love'?" I took a slurp through my straw but a delayed snort of disdain transported a lump of banana up my nose.

As I floundered, Jennifer wagged a triumphant finger at me. "Serves you right. You mocked the cards. The cards will get their revenge."

"What exactly are the cards supposed to achieve? Because so far, they seem to be creating disharmony."

"They just give you something to think about. Mel's got a pack and she takes one out each morning and it's like a theme for the day."

"Melanie? What does she want with this kind of magic? I thought she was in harmony with the universe and knew all its secrets."

Jennifer's ex had been teaching yoga for over a year, after abandoning a stressful career as a maths teacher. She had chilled out enough to let Jen give me keys to their house. However, in today's spirit of false jollity, she was fair game. There was a smell hanging over us as we clutched our badges of wealth and parried our wit. It was the smell of stale piss, lingering in our nostrils along with the banana.

The smell had followed us from shop to shop, as a middle-aged guy in dark and voluminous clothing kept enquiring of shopkeepers whether he could buy a crystal. At last, he found what he wanted in the shop where Jennifer bought the Angel Cards, and headed for the counter with snot hanging in a viscous stream from his nose to the tip of his beard.

His voice had the resonance and volume of an actor on the stage of the RSC: "I'm homeless, and I've saved my money to buy a crystal. It's like a precious stone, isn't it?" He held up his chosen pebble.

The guy behind the counter was of the heavy metal/new age hybrid but with the serious features of a bookshop assistant.

"Yes," he said. "It is a precious stone."

The customer let a pile of pound coins and fifty-pence pieces fall from his dirty hand on to the counter and the assistant selected a few and left the rest, saying, "That's your change." (Not "Woah man, too much bread!") When the man left, another assistant lit a joss stick, with only the smallest smile.

"What do you think?" I asked Jennifer in the refuge of World of Juice. "Is there something wrong with a society where a ragged homeless man saves his money to buy a polished stone?"

"Maybe it will protect him."

I couldn't tell if she was joking; but then, I just didn't know the party line on this one. "Did it make you feel uncomfortable, though? I mean, he needed clothes and a bath, not a ritual cleansing."

"You know what, Joss? It's his money. Want to take it off him and buy him a can of Tennants?"

I gave up and let her shepherd me to Muji. We went home without an outfit for the Magazineland awards, but with £100 of smart and timeless home accessories. Smoothie-related expenditure had robbed me of an astonishing £15 and we had given £5 between us to beggars. What if we had given £100 to beggars and £15 to Muji? What if we had given smoothies to beggars, or even a handy pocket pack of Angel Cards? Should we have bought that crystal for that man so he could save his money for Tennants? As

I sat up late at night in a corner of my studio, spliffing away and staring at the shiny new vases and candle holders that I didn't need, I thought of all the times that day when something different could have happened.

Then I sneaked a hand into the pocket of Jennifer's trousers – not difficult as they were draped over the arm of my chair. I had to hold the little card up to the beam of orange light that shone between the curtains, but then I could see a crude picture of two angels, face to face, holding hands, and a single word: "Truth".

Lucky for us both, she was already asleep.

Private chat 3

<amy~> hey!

<CustardSlice> Hey sweetheart.

<amy~> i been thinkin bout u girl

<CustardSlice> Uh-huh. Me too. Bout you.

<amy~> u have to tell me yr name now

<CustardSlice> Oh I do, do I? It's Joss.

<amy~> JOSS. i like that. cute name. why did u make me w8?

<CustardSlice> Why do I make u w8 for anything? Because it keeps you close.

<amy~> hmmm. some argument

<CustardSlice> You talkin back girl?

<amy~> who me?

<amy~> y'know, custard slice aint such a hot name now. joss *is* a hot name. you want to think about that b4 u hook yr next girl

<CustardSlice> What next girl?? UR the only one, babe :)

<amy~> cept your real-life gf, right?

<CustardSlice> Yeah. Dont spoil it.

<amy~> would i?

<CustardSlice> Let me spoil *you*. Get over here.

5
function

Self-diagnosis

For a long time, I thought I had mild manic depression, or mild bipolar illness, to use the latest terminology. I wasn't happy with this definition because it didn't feel mild to me. But I had never been hospitalised; and no one else perceived me as manic depressive, whether mild or extreme – rather, they kept telling me that manic depressives were really really mad, not like me at all. So it must be mild.

What delighted me about the illness known as cyclothymia, when I first discovered it, was that it precisely described my own "rapid cycling" and inexplicable mood swings in a separate category of their own. Part of the definition was that the patient wasn't fucked enough to go to hospital, but hey, she was mad enough to get in the manual. And this kind of patient did have infrequent "euthymic" periods, when she felt fine, just like me. Yip, I was that patient.

Many was the happy/sad day I spent reading and rereading the definitions, clinical criteria and symptoms of cyclothymia. Like the illness itself, my interest in this material was cyclical. I would become obsessed with it for a time, spending hours on the net in the dysfunctional communities of bipolar people, who were prone

to irritability as much as empathy, insult as much as intuitive connection. They were also plagued by an abusive man who didn't
seem to have bipolar at all, but posted constantly and was accused
by others of being a Scientologist, possibly the worst slander
known to Usenet and certainly one from which it is hard to re-
cover. This particular user, whom I will not dignify with a name,
split into several people with similar names, all of whom accused
each other of being the usurper. Court action was always about to
be taken. The other members could not help but be drawn in. A
simple post called "Ignore him!" might advise, "If we all ignore
him – and you know who I mean – then he will go bother some
other group." This would turn into the biggest discussion of the
day and everyone would have to give their opinion, including
Himself and all his other selves. Fortunately, bipolar being what it
is, everyone would post and post their vehement and articulate
contributions and then a new distraction would come along and
they would throw themselves into that with equal gusto.

I liked the community feeling from hanging out where everyone had severe mood swings, but I didn't like the way they all insisted that without treatment this would get worse and worse until
the patient killed herself. They were all on medication and
thought I was very wrong for seeing a homeopath and for self-
prescribing cannabis (which incidentally seemed to be unavailable
across great swathes of the US). I veered between believing them –
and panicking that I would be dead by 50 – and trying to convert
them to my way of thinking – not easy when most were sicker
than me and knew they could not survive without medication.
(One person who started sending me personal emails in admira-
tion of my campaign was later accused of Scientological leanings
and ostracised.)

There were similarities between my attraction to the bipolar label and my attraction to lesbian identity back in the 80s. Indeed, I could see many connections between mental illness and sexual identity, not least the fact that dykes were/are so prone to madness. Then there seemed to my mind to be a particular link between gender dysphoria and depression. My FTM friend Ludlow found his depression lifted as he moved to his new identity. His psychiatrist got him to track his moods every hour on a chart. I tried doing the same on a calendar but there wasn't room.

Just as some straight people think you can't help being a lesbian, that you were born that way, and others think you could snap out of it if you chose – and just as most dykes think gender dysphoria is a form of bull-headed ignorance about socialised gender norms – so opinion among my friends (straight and gay) was divided as to my madness. But most of them thought I should stop dwelling on it and get on with my life.

If I went to the doctor and got myself diagnosed with cyclothymia, would they feel differently? It was hard to know. I hadn't made much effort to convince Jennifer. She didn't like to think of my symptoms as symptoms, she liked to think of them as my flawed and difficult personality, and the furthest she went was the occasional declaration that there was "something wrong with me", usually retracted under questioning. (Yet she'd had no problem diagnosing Madam as schizophrenic. It seemed you were only mentally ill if the symptoms made other people feel really pissed off and/or sorry for you for a prolonged period.)

One evening, I showed her the clinical criteria for cyclothymia, including short mood cycles, dramatic swings in self-esteem and productivity, "irritable-angry-explosive outbursts that alienate loved ones", and "uninhibited people-seeking" or promiscuity alternating with introverted self-absorption. Not forgetting the drug use, the insomnia, the over-sleeping and the over-spending...

Jennifer looked up from *Touched with Fire: Manic-depressive illness and the artistic temperament* by Kay Redfield Jamison. "Joss!" She was laughing. "This isn't an illness. Everyone is different on different days, for God's sake. How is that mental illness? Do you actually think this is what you've got: Cyc-lo-thy-mia?" She elongated the word as if its unusualness proved its uselessness, an odd strategy for a scientist, but then, the mocking-loving combo was one of her specialities.

I harumphed. I was trying not to cry. How could she understand the relief and delight of seeing all your symptoms in easy-to-follow categories on one page of a book? She couldn't. And yet I had expected her to. I had even thought she might want to join the internet support network for people with cyclothymic partners. (Why did I think that, when she refused to check her email from one day to the next?)

"What's this about promiscuity, anyway?" she asked. "Is there something you're not telling me?"

Kind of, I thought. "No," I said, swallowing down my disappointment in her. "Never mind, give it here, I shouldn't have shown you." This was precisely why I had never shown her before, though God knows I had tried to explain enough times.

"Is this why you cried at the fairies and elves party?" She waited eagerly for my nod as if she had finally cracked the Secret of Joss. So, now I had what I wanted, for her to share the secret; but to her, the secret was a JOKE. "Ooooo-kaaaaay. You weren't in the mood for uninhibited people-seeking? Or fairy-seeking?" She giggled. She actually giggled. Oh, she was in her element now and had no idea that I was on my way to an irritable-angry-explosive outburst that would alienate my loved one.

I had a vision of myself at this year's fairies and elves party (an annual event organised by Flic and Ali's crowd in aid of the softball team). I was throwing my body about the dancefloor to the 60s/70s/80s tunes of DJ Mike, in my green shirt and trousers, with a woolly hat pulled down behind my ears to make them stick out and a tuft of hair at the front. Jennifer photographed me with two other elves because she thought we looked like Snap, Crackle and Pop. I went up to someone I didn't know and admired her Wicked Fairy costume. I was seeking elves and fairies in an uninhibited way until about 11 o'clock when I felt a period of introverted self-absorption coming upon me and started to cry. Jennifer had taken me outside and held me to her, not complaining as green face-paint smeared its way across the shoulder of her white fairy dress.

"So," she said now, "it wasn't the drink then, it was the, er, psychiatric disorder? How d'you say it? Cyclomythia?"

"Something like that," I mumbled, "yeah, that's close enough." I couldn't really blame her for getting the word wrong, even though it was probably an unconscious pun on the word "myth", but I could blame her for getting the tone wrong, for misunderstanding. And I would blame her for some time, harbouring a grudge while she was channel-surfing that made me veto every programme until she turned the set off, kissed me on the neck and moaned. I was surprised that she had got to the moaning so soon after the channel-surfing. Didn't she need to adjust to the new activity? I certainly did.

And I wasn't about to forgive her, even as her hand pushed its way between my legs with the kind of familiarity that only comes after too long together. There was a whingeing chorus in my head: Why don't you love me? Why don't you love me? And still the heart remains a child. Etc. She could shove her whole fucking arm up me (and she would, if I didn't assert myself first) but I wouldn't stop feeling that she didn't care enough. I had waited weeks for sex and now I had to accept it when and how she fancied, or wait a few more weeks. Was that fair? Her other hand reached under my shirt... My resistance began to melt... And just as I moaned, "Oh, fuck me then, you slag," there was a knock at the door.

"Sorry to bother you, Joss," said Madam, "but did they tell you when my makeover will be started properly? Only they came and moved everything around and then –"

"You have interesting timing," I said, pulling down on my T-shirt so it covered the fly of my boxer shorts.

"It's not my fault," she replied. "They said 9am and then they arrived at 11 and then –"

"That's not what I meant... Look, ring us at the office tomorrow and I'll see what I can find out, OK?"

"All right then, thank you. Is Jennifer there?"

"Er, yes."

"Can I come in and say hello?"

"No. I mean, it's not really a good time now."

"Oh, all right. Night-night then."

"Goodnight."

She called through the crack in the door: "Night-night, Jennifer!"

I shut the door and turned to the bed, where my love was lounging luxuriously in her underwear. "She's a nutcase," I said.

"Well, in the light of this evening's discussion, that's an interesting claim. She is a nutcase why? Does she get more sleep on

Saturday nights than on Sundays? Does she sometimes want to leave a party early? Has she ever spent too much on a blouse?"

"When did you start talking like this? Where's the woman I fell in love with, who hated sarcasm?"

"That wasn't sarcasm. That was a high form of irony."

"Shit, you've caught it off me." I pulled her bra down to get at her tits and sucked one after another into my mouth while we both giggled. Ah, the smugness of the long-term dysfunctional couple.

The Maggies

We took our seats at the *Modern Interiors* table. The banqueting hall was huge and the chandeliers were only outdone by the massive loudspeakers banked at either side of the stage. "Things Can Only Get Better" was playing out of these speakers as if we were at a New Labour rally.

I was wearing Drew's late father's dinner jacket after an emergency appeal to her wardrobe; my colleagues were all in the full evening wear appropriate to their gender. Our leader, Caroline Chatterby, looked almost beautiful in her red off-the-shoulder gown, while Tim had also scrubbed up nicely in his evening suit. The art director, Lesley, was wearing an understated black velvet number to which she had pinned a big piece of chunky silver jewellery, and her long hair was up.

Altogether, there were about twenty of us on the mag, including Clare, who was a few seats away from me and seemed as unsure as me of how our relationship should play in this setting.

A waiter poured our champagne as the song changed to "We Are the Champions". Clearly the night was to have an inspirational theme. If they cued up "Three Lions on a Shirt", though, I might have to make my excuses.

"Are there any songs about magazines?" I asked Tim, who was sitting to my left, drinking down his fizz like lemonade.

"Hmm." He seemed pleased by the laddish question. But then, I had had some years to fine-tune myself to his interests, albeit mainly by electronic mail.

"Let's see," he pondered. "Do you mean *really* about magazines, or could be taken to be about them?"

"Really about, for ten points each; could be taken to be about, five points each."

He passed on this teaser to those sitting nearby and the entries rolled in immediately. Geoff the designer (his long hair in a pony-tail, a string cowboy tie round his neck) was tunelessly trying to string together some Americanese: "Mah home from home lover blah blah she was pure like a thingy, no one could ever take, blah blah, thingy is a CENNERFOLD!"

"My blood runs cold," cringed his boss, Lesley.

"Here's one," said Chatterbox. She took a deep breath and sang out: "On the cover of a maag-azine!"

"What's that from?" asked Tim, faux innocent.

"I'm not sure," she replied brightly, in party mode. No one was about to help her out so she was awarded nulle points.

"But it's a real song," she whinged, unheeded, before drifting despondently loowards.

"Yo, ho, she's mah LADY, yeah weah, special LADY…" This was Geoff again, shaking his head like a muppet till his ponytail slapped him in the face.

"*Woman*," crooned Tim, inspired, "I know you un-der-stand, the little *shite* inside a man…"

It could not be long before someone recognised the Eezy-Play version of this game: many of our own Magazineland titles were also songs, from accidents such as "Cars" and "Bicycle" to "Here Comes the Bride". But there was to be no such epiphany, for the music and the lights were fading and an announcer's voice came over the speakers.

"Ladies and gentlemen, your host for the evening, Laviniaaaa Buuuuuff-Jones!"

Everyone clapped as a small woman of middle years stalked on-stage in a glittery dress, carrying a live pug in a diamond collar. Up to now, I had never seen our publishing director in the flesh. The night's inspirational theme was dented by her schoolmarm attitude: though she welcomed us to the annual Magazineland awards for outstanding achievement, she also cautioned that heckling and discourtesy would not be treated lightly. I was so tempted to heckle at that moment that I had to distract myself by reading the order of ceremonies on the card in front of me. Half the awards would be presented before dinner; Hannah's mag was up for the one just after pud. Looking around, I glimpsed her some distance across the room, in a flowered dress I recognised from her birthday do. I waved but she shook her head, almost imperceptibly. Clearly she saw the situation as akin to Founders' Day at school, where no movement was permitted.

But even as I thought this, Tim was swinging the champagne bottle in my direction and saying quite audibly, "Never mind the bollocks, give us the Bolly!"

"Yeah, fill her up!" I encouraged him. "Are we likely to win anything tonight, boss?"

"Well, we have put in for Best Production Values but there seems to be some doubt as to whether our leader managed to fill in the form correctly."

"Yeah," cried Clare, who had Wonderwoman hearing, "I had to put it right!"

"That sounds about right for Caroline," I said, before turning back to Tim. "Best Production Values, though, that might even include the subs, eh?"

"Well, the artroom will probably think it just means them, but we must ask ourselves, do designers have values? Or do they just have pictures and layouts? Surely design is without values, whereas subbing might be defined as the pursuit of values, indeed, of production values? Isn't it the subs who keep the artroom in line, who send the pages off so that the magazine gets *produced*?"

"These are excellent arguments, Timmy, but who gets the award?"

"The art director."

"As I thought. Cheers."

We clinked glasses and he said, "The medal is theirs, my friend, but the glory is ours."

People were shushing us and, on the stage, Ms Buff-Jones had stopped speaking and was shaking her head at Tim. Apparently, though we were halfway down the hall, we were making so much noise that it constituted one of her discourtesies. I wondered if we would be evicted. And I needed the toilet. What would happen if I got up?

I drank some more champagne.

Even though it happened every year, I had hoped I would not find myself swept along by the worshipping of Mammon. But that night, in that banqueting hall, with that champagne, I was high. Oh, not immediately. When Buffy (as the boys were calling her) barked out the nominations for Best New Concept, I mocked the way someone from IT had been put forward for thinking up a corporate mousemat theme; but I gaped as pictures of the nominees flashed up on giant TV screens. The company had certainly "gone large" this year. The male announcer's disembodied voice suddenly boomed out, telling us about each person as if they were on *The Price Is Right.*

"Des is 27 and lives in Barnet with his wife and two kids. He has been with the company for four years and luuurves the 22nd floor. He is known to the staff of the Kwikeetz for his daily sausage sandwich with ketchup *and* mayo, and Des says that he had his idea for the mousemats while taking a tour of the building and seeing how many people were using *magazines* as mousemats. Hey kids! That's not cool!"

According to Laura V Neuberg, author of *The Delicate Soul: Getting by in today's rough world*, this is the kind of situation that delicate souls should manage carefully. I know I am a delicate soul because of my high scores in her self-testing quiz. I scored 37 out of 48, and a score of 24 or more indicates that you are probably delicate. But then, "if only one or two questions are true of you but they are *extremely* true, you might also be justified in calling yourself delicate." (Oh boy, did Jennifer love this book.)

The DS is so sensitive to noise, light, bustle, and all-round party atmosphere, that she may mistake her excitement for fear or anxiety, as her heart pumps away and she breaks out in a dizzy sweat. However, if she treats herself nicely and says to herself (to paraphrase), "My, it is exciting here, with all these people and so much going on," then she might realise she's going to be OK. Should this tactic fail, I am pleased to say that the DS is fully entitled to take herself home to bed.

Not that I wanted to go home to bed, but there was certainly a lot going on for me as the special music started for the winner of the first award to go up to the podium. A follow-spot tracked his way through the crowd and people were clapping enthusiastically. His colleagues from his table were on their feet, cheering and shouting his name as if he had won the war, or at least an MBE. Buffy cracked a smile but it soon faded because the cheering had gone on too long for her liking. The mousemat man was awarded a curious trophy: a hologram of a magazine. But he was as delighted as if he'd been given a bucket of chocolates.

Well, by the time they got on to the third award, I was whooping with the best of them and swaying to the music and shouting out "Good on ya" to the winner.

"Isn't it fantastic?" I said to Tim.

"What?"

I threw out my arms. "All this!"

"And salmon mousse!" he said.

In fact the salmon was poached and the mousse, when it arrived, was chocolate. Tim came back from the toilets rubbing his nose and saying "Nice one" to Geoff. He might as well have clinked his coffee spoon against his glass to get the attention of the room and declared, "I've just had a lovely line of charlie." He sat down a satisfied man, but his face lit up further when he saw that someone had bought him a cigar. He struck a match, looking around the table, trying to guess who was his stogy angel. And then he took a puff and smiled.

"Socialism…" he said to everyone and no one, raising his champagne flute. "Dontcha just love it?"

When Hannah's mag won Most Improved New Small Profit Centre, there was some dissent in the hall. My sister's team were all smiling proudly as the spotlight followed them down the aisle – it seemed impossible for anyone to greet their own success with irony or disinterest. My table were cheering raucously, but more than one voice from the back was calling out "Fix!" Sour grapes from the less glamorous new titles on the shortlist: *Gifted Baby* and *Eat Your Greens*.

"Good Year for the Roses" was the theme chosen by the invisible DJ to celebrate *The Outside Room*'s success, and Elvis C's miserable rendition all but obscured the boos. Buffy was displeased with the negativity. "A tremendous success!" she screeched, less in congratulation to the team before her than condemnation of the dissenters. The pug grunted from the lectern, its black eyes and pink tongue all protruding.

Hannah and her pals joined hands and waved them in the air like sportspeople as Buffy presented a hologram to the *OR* publisher, who just happened to be her lover, as Tim was now explaining.

"Oh, that's why they're shouting 'Fix!'"

"Sure is. It's also why he's allowed to pursue his dream of elitism with his posh gardens mag, while the rest of us are forced to pander to the masses."

"How come you know all this?"

"How come you don't?" He looked genuinely puzzled.

"Er... 'cos you never tell me anything?"

"Oh right, sorry." He poured some more champagne.

My head was as light and airy as one of those Manhattan apartments we used to feature in the magazine and my alcohol alarm was ringing loudly, yet I accepted more champagne every time it came my way. And something else was coming my way: Clare, whom I had blocked out all night, hoping she would keep her distance. Friend/e-flirt/colleague is not an easy combination to manage, especially for the cyclothymic lesbian. But now she was sitting next to me in her flattering dress which showed just enough cleavage to put the word "cleavage" into a person's mind without them necessarily thinking "tits on show!" It's a gauge without a name (unless there is a secret femme name that I haven't been told) but an important one.

They were announcing the award that we were up for. The room fell silent and, other than nodding, I was not required to acknowledge Clare's proximity. But she shifted her chair so that her leg was comfortably brushing mine, as if we were lovers.

Yes, I was distracted, but I registered Lesley rising from her seat with a modest smile and – more modest still – inviting Tim to go up with her to receive the award for Production Values.

"Let's all go!" he insisted, drunkenly, and suddenly the whole artroom and the whole subs' desk were on their feet and heading for the stage. But Clare had not understood that she was not among the honoured. As I made my way up the aisle, she was holding my hand like a child who has been told not to let go. Should I shake her off? It would be rude and she wouldn't know why I'd done it. Instead, I let her trail me to the stage where we all made a line like kids in a ballet display and watched our leaders being given a hologram of a magazine.

The scene had taken on a disturbing glow and I realised that my eyes were failing me, that my body was just a vessel for champagne and its normal functions were shutting down. I tried to tell Clare but she wouldn't let go of my hand and was stroking it as we left the stage, stumbling down the steps and crashing into our colleagues. I wrenched my hand from hers and made a break for the toilets. There I sat on the loo with my head against the wall and fell asleep.

I was woken by Clare banging on the door and telling me it was time to boogie. She wouldn't go away till I emerged, doused my face in cold water and allowed her to lead me to the dancefloor. And what a disturbing sight that was, like a convention for businesspeople who lacked the dancing gene. Suits humping themselves everywhere. Clare seemed to want to get off with me. I wanted to go home. I was panicking, which is far worse when I'm drunk because I can't think how to get myself home. Instead I was dancing with my best friend's girlfriend while she rubbed her hands over my bum – surely the butch's job. And then I was hyperventilating... And then I was sitting on the floor while people danced on around me and Clare shouted down at me that I was no fun. Did she kick me, or did I just expect her to? I remember lying flat on my back with the disco lights whirring in my eyes.

I honestly don't think I got off with her.

May the Lord make us truly thankful

Giving in has its own rewards. I was now officially off sick and could take some time to stare at the ceiling and see projected on it the many manic and depressed episodes of my life and consider the various symptoms I had experienced at those times and compare them to the text books (and to Sally Field in *ER*).

My panic mode included a fast heartbeat and confused thinking. It was a fight or flight response, but neither fight nor flight ensued – rather, a kind of paralysis set in. Sitting on the floor at the Maggies was pretty typical, although alcohol had contributed to that particular episode and on other occasions I had managed to get myself out of the door into the fresh air before the onset of the tears, the desperate sobbing that prevented my finding a way home.

Then there was the depression, the most severe version being the one I was now experiencing: inability to move from bed or to think about anything else. Pain in my chest or solar plexus would lead to "self-holding" in which the patient (as I thought of myself) held her arms or hands across the place that hurt, as one might with a headache. And I would cry. I would cry for most of the day and part of the night. I might stop for a while but I would start again as soon as I noticed I had stopped crying and was feeling a bit better. (This was often worse at night, particularly between 3 and 6am, also known as the dark night of the soul or The Learning Zone.)

And then there was the mania, which I had experienced so recently but which now seemed so foreign. That time when the thoughts won't stop and the words won't stop and the talking won't stop... and if a person was able to paint, the painting wouldn't stop either.

But modes could switch at any time. Known technically as "rapid cycling", these sudden switches could happen within minutes, could take me tumbling into desperate sadness or flying up into spiritual enlightenment, all within the hour.

It was more than a change of mood; it felt like a change of personality, body, mind, being. And during a particularly rapid cycle, I would have incessant thoughts about the mood, the last mood and the change, and the way that other people must be feeling about these changes. Telling myself to stop it might have a delaying effect but nothing more. Saying to myself, for instance, "There's no need to be sad, you are at a nice party with people you like," might work for minutes but probably no longer, and the effort of keeping back the welling sadness meant that when it burst forth it was both a terrible disappointment/failure and a massive release.

Yes, I knew that everyone had moods. My friends made sure I knew it, whenever I raised the subject of my supposed mental illness. But while other people might feel like they were going mad for three days before their period, or when their grandmother died or when they were persecuted by their boss, I felt that way quite a lot of the time. Believe me (oh won't someone believe me?), you know when you're mad.

Had I always had these symptoms? As a baby I would lie quietly in my pram in the garden, looking at my hands in front of my face. I wasn't one of these that have crying fits that last all night. I wasn't born with cyclothymia, or if I was, it was dormant, as is proper, till later (the books said the illness came on in the teens or early adulthood). But how much later?

I started playgroup by hiding in a tea-chest for the whole session, safe. But I didn't stay there every time. I enjoyed making art: butterflies from paint splodges; a teddy carriage from a cardboard box that I dragged home with William Ted joggling upright like an uncomfortable king.

In the Infants, I did not mix with the other children, I mixed with the dinner ladies. I acquired a dispensation to sit in the head-mistress's office and paint pictures at morning break. At junior school I only watched, until I made a special friend with whom to draw maps of the playground and fly from benches in our duffel coats (must do up chinstrap to enable flight) and do the rounds of the marble pitches. I avoided gangs or joining in with other games. I could put this down to being a baby butch, to the gen-dered nature of the games, but I will get myself into one more bi-nary argument: Not Proper Girl. More likely, I was scared of the children.

It was "the best school in the area", streamed from age seven or eight by social class and ethnicity. We may have taken a biased test or the teachers may simply have drawn up a chart of who deserved a chance in life, I don't know. But I was middle class and deserved a chance and, with it, a centrally heated classroom in the main building and dinner with grace at 12.30 prompt. Not for me an out-of-the-way prefab and a late lunch, or the indignity of the rough and rushed *third* sitting for those with sandwiches or free dinners. Better for a top-streamer to skip dinner than chance third sitting, where children with darting eyes would pick you out while those with no money or no friends or no English sat in ones and twos in silence. No one led grace at third sitting. You had to find your own.

I acquired the best teachers (or perhaps the teachers whose accents most resembled the Queen's English) and a belief that poor people want to kill you for your dinner.

But, while the boys who didn't understand were beaten with pumps and the girls who cheated lost house points, those with new uniforms and bright ideas were encouraged. I don't remember being particularly unhappy until I acquired even more privilege – until I started private school. Suddenly, ideas were no longer rewarded. Learning was rewarded. Fun was out and seriousness was in. And as I became cheekier, playing for laughs and excitement with my commentary, burly spinster teachers would take me outside, roll up their sleeves and choose from a range of questions that might as well have been chalked on the wall above my head:

"What is the matter with you?"

"What would your mother think?"

"Is something wrong at home?"

Something is wrong right here. I am in a prison serving a seven-year term and I will soon take to thumping my friends to keep their attention. I wasn't actually thinking any of this and I was still too polite to think "fuck off". I was thinking: "Get away you scary horrible woman, get away from me."

Whenever I pass a school now, as an adult, I say a little prayer: Thank you Lord for delivering me from school, watch over your children as they suffer there now.

*

I have trouble distinguishing one year of my teens from another but I know I found places where I wasn't weird: a group of kids who were putting together a comic; Youth CND (with its screenings of the end of the world, like a sermon on hell for atheists, inducing terror of burning eyeballs and a resolution to be good and convert others to the cause); an indie nightclub on seven floors, full of Goths and New Romantics, Bowie lookalikes and Mods; the controlled chaos of a campsite on the Yorkshire coast with a bunch of these mates – all spiked hair and spiked cider.

But was I all right or was something missing even then? Lying on my bed playing the Beatles White Album, burning candles and incense and making drawings for an abstract mural… I'd say there was something missing all right – a big fat spliff. I was living the drug culture without the drugs. The cider was spiked with rum, not Class As, and when a joint did come my way, I waved it away. I didn't know I was going to learn to love it.

But at least I was making art.

I had ample time to think about all this after Drew had signed me off work for a fortnight. I felt guilty asking her to do it, in the circumstances, but it was either that or visit my GP, a man who had once told me he was a lesbian (don't ask).

So, I was under the care of the same doctor who tended to my "mad" neighbour. And being at home for days on end meant that I could hear the soundtrack to that neighbour's makeover.

My employer was now responsible for most of the money coming into my house, what with Madam's new decor and my sick pay. And money was coming in all the time. Delivery vans kept stopping in the middle of the road with their hazards flashing as bright pink furniture was unloaded and bumped up the stairs.

Maybe they were photographing different combos or pretending the room was bigger than it was, I don't know, but there sure was a lot of stuff.

Sir Lancelot was there nearly every day and more than once I heard him lose patience with her. When he handed over to some workmen, she helped them paint, they laughed at her handiwork and she swore at them. Through all of this, I kept asking myself why I had let it happen. But I could always fall back on the fact that she had asked for it in the first place.

Apart from the paint fumes and strains of Madonna seeping under my door – and through the holes in the wall under the sink – the process barely inconvenienced me, though I was once called upon to choose between two patterned duvet covers, neither of which felt like 100% cotton.

At least it was keeping her busy during my thinking time. Drew had told me not to "over-think", but then, she didn't know what had happened between Clare and me at the Maggies. Instead, I had played up the Amy angle with her: how I was obsessed with Amy and couldn't think about anyone else and even when I was with Jen, I was thinking about Amy.

It's weird, but at the time, there's no backing off from it. You can say to yourself, "I wonder if all of this is just a distraction from sorting out my primary relationship?" You can say, "I can't possibly love her, I don't know her," or "She's not mine to love," or "I'm not available and I have to stop thinking about her," or whatever, but obsession cannot be controlled by logic. The body remembers what it wants, it does not let you forget. The mind deals in contradictions, that is what it's for. It can keep a rational argument going in a small front portion while the mid and back sections brew chemicals to pump around the body, sex obsession chemicals.

*

Clare's body rubs against me from behind – I melt – I want her – I want to turn and press my mouth to hers – stop that – I must phone Jen and ask her – don't think – I want Amy here next to me now in my arms – fantasy – melting – what – people have affairs every day and no one needs to know – there are lots of girls online to distract you from the ones you're obsessed with and you don't have to get obsessed with everyone you meet and there is more to life than sex and – more to life than books you know but not much more – Clare has beautiful blue eyes – she looks right inside me she wants me and she would beg in bed – phone Jen – think about it think about it think about *it* – Amy loves me she says so she says I love it when you fuck me Joss fuck me – put your hands in her pants see how wet you are thinking about them all all in bed together just for you they love each other because you want them to and they will kiss each other and look at you and you feel no guilt they are all in it together they want to make you happy like a man

Private chat 4

Amy has plenty to do: her school work, the job in the copy shop that funds it. And she goes out to bars with her friends, dances salsa with Terri... But she doesn't have a girl other than Joss. She has feelings for Joss that she's never had for a cyberdate before.

It's good that Joss is in England because otherwise she would be a real distraction. Take tonight. Amy can barely focus on making a snack because her eye is on the clock as it ticks towards seven. Seven here, midnight in London, England – their appointed time every Monday, no matter what else goes on in the week, no matter whether they email in between or not, have cyber in between or not. She has it all in her head as a pattern but it has only been three weeks – three intense weeks, like falling in love. Today, at work, Amy felt her face flush when a butch boygirl who looked like her vision of Joss came in the shop with a flyer to be duplicated. And she walked home with scenes from last Thursday's cyberdate playing in her head that made her knees weak – she had to stop and bring her breathing under control, stop thinking about Joss's ever-hard silicone dick inside her and the way she said, "Tell me you like that, look down into my eyes babe, mmm, let your tits brush my face, oh jeeeesus..."

7pm. Log on.

Temptation

To the puzzled doctor, it felt a little like a home visit, with Joss immobile on the bed, covered in a fluffy blanket on which were littered soggy tissues. It was thankfully rare, however, to find a patient's home in such a mess. Joss's entire wardrobe was on the floor, forming a sea of colourful cotton and fleece, the width of the room, to a variable depth of around a foot, with Airwalks and Vans poking their suede toes up to the surface here and there. Newspapers and magazines were in piles all round the bed, to the height of the bed, as if to ward off predators. Dirty dishes and cups were stacked in the sink, next to the sink, on the cluttered bedside table, and even, in what seemed to be the most recent development, on the floor next to the bed, balanced on top of the newspapers and clothes. There was a smell like a blocked sink. The cafetiere was white and grey with mould.

But Drew was not put off by these surroundings, as long as she continued to think of it as a home visit rather than an evening with her best friend. (On a home visit, the doctor would certainly not offer to wash up.) And she was doing her best to understand.

"So you're saying you're in love with this woman that you've never met?" she ventured.

"Fuck, fuck, fuck." The patient looked around the studio as if she might find the answer in the chaos. "I don't know. I'm obsessed with her and I want to meet her and I think about her all the time. Last night, Jennifer was falling asleep with her head on my chest – which is about as intimate as we get right now – and I couldn't get rid of this vision of what me and this woman had done online the night before..."

"You're not going to tell me what that was, are you?"

"I don't think that would be appropriate." Joss finally cracked a smile. "What am I going to do?"

"You have to stop doing it, the cyber thing. You have to stop talking to her. Is that what you call it? Talking?"

"Yeah, whatever. Talking, seeing, fucking." She groaned.

"Maybe you should ask Clare about it. She used to do this cybersex thing too, you know."

Joss stared at her for a second as if this was news, then looked away. "Right. But I'm asking you."

"Well, I don't really get it, Joss, to be honest with you. You've never met her. I mean, you say you've had sex but sex involves, like, being in the same room at the same time."

"It is like sex, though. In some ways it's more spiritual because you're on another plane, outside the body. And in some ways it's more physical... It's hard to explain. You're so focused and connected."

"So it's better than sex? So why do you want to meet her in real life?"

"Because it's gone so far now. It's just what has to happen next."

"Jesus, listen to yourself." Drew leaned forward in her chair. "*Nothing* has to happen next. What about Jennifer?"

"I know. Do you think I should tell her?"

"No!" yelled Drew. "I've told you what you should do: ditch the internet girl and commit yourself to your real-life flesh and blood girlfriend. This whole episode is just a distraction, to fuck things up with Jennifer."

"How do you know that? How do you know I'm not meant to be with this other woman?"

"Doh! She isn't even a woman, she's just some words on a computer screen. She might be a man or a robot or a typing monkey for all you know."

"I think I can tell the difference between a dyke and a monkey."

"She might be one of those bisexual bonobos. They're highly intelligent."

"She's not a monkey. She looks like a bit like that nice paramedic off *ER*."

"Oh, you've seen a picture."

Joss played with the corner of her blanket. "No, she just told me she looks like her."

"Right."

"Well, you've got to admit it's an odd comparison to choose if it's made up. I mean, it's not even a famous person…"

"Probably just his favourite lesboid programme. With the Carrie plotline and all."

"It's not a man! She's not a monkey or a man!"

"And you know that how?"

"I don't have to prove it to you. She would have sent a pic but I didn't want to break the spell."

"Yeah, good point," Drew said sarcastically. "So what about you? Did *you* send a picture, or invoke a looky-likey?"

Joss glanced around the room once more. Eventually she muttered something under her breath.

"I beg your pardon?" asked Drew.

"I told her I looked like Robbie Williams."

Drew guffawed. "And what did she say to that?"

"She didn't know who he was."

"Oh, she's going up in my estimation. OK, let's assume she is the gorgeous young black dyke about town that you believe."

"That's big of you."

"And very exotic."

"What?"

"Oh come on, Joss. She lives in New York, your dream city. She's black and you've never gone out with anyone black –"

"I have! In sixth form, a guy I met at a disco. He –"

"You know what I mean. Your boring long-term girlfriend's white and all your boring close friends. I suppose she has piercings all over and hangs out in some trendy bar in Greenwich Village and writes like she's sending a text message?"

Joss looked stung. "You've been talking to Clare."

"You told all this to Clare and not to me?"

"You *haven't* been talking to Clare?"

"I'm just describing the opposite of Jennifer, actually."

"The opposite of Jennifer would be –"

"Your internet friend."

"Not. Anyway, I can't believe you're so focused on her being 'different'. I pity your patients if that's how you're categorising everyone. Oh, a boring white person, a thrilling black person..."

"Are you being deliberately dense?" Drew got up to pace the room but did not get far, wading through sweatshirts. She kicked her way towards the bed. "I'm saying that *you're* exoticising her. You –"

"I know what you're saying, thank you. And you wouldn't be saying it if you didn't think she sounded exotic to you. Well, we got talking online without knowing anything about each other and it wasn't her blackness or her piercings that brought us together, actually. It was our sense of humour and our above-average intelligence in a room full of idiots. Yes, she is an exciting person, but she thinks the same about me. Christ, I don't exactly live a conventional life here. Look around you."

Drew didn't need to look around. "I'm standing in your unconventional life and it makes me think a little convention would do you no harm."

"Why are you so angry with me?"

"Because you won't help yourself!"

"I can't."

"OK, whatever."

"Will you stop saying that? You've got that off Clare, haven't you?"

"What?"

"That 'whatever' thing that she does. It's infuriating."

"Oh right, now I'm infuriating. Ha bloody ha." They were silent for some time. Then Drew thought of her bed and heard herself saying: "Well, I have to go home, kiddo. Early start tomorrow, healing the sick and all that."

"There is something else I wanted to ask you, Doc. Do you think I should tell them at work about Madam's condition? So they know not to wind her up? Only the makeover seems to be taking forever and –"

"Can't discuss a patient with you – as you well know. Why don't you just concentrate on sorting yourself out? Have you ditched every single one of your therapists?"

"Can we talk about that some other time?"

Drew nodded, said her goodbyes and let herself out, coming face to face with Madam in the hall.

"Oh, hello, Doctor Drew!" cried the redhead, with such glee that Drew suspected she had carefully timed the encounter. "Is Joss all right? I'm a bit worried about her."

"She's fine, fine. And how are you?"

"Oh, I'm fine, I'm really well, Doctor. I'm going to come and see you soon."

"Good, good. Stay well."

"I'm having a makeover. In my flat. Do you want to come and see it?"

"Oh, I can see it there, through the door, lovely. Nice wall-paper, very good, very good."

As Drew dived for the car, she decided to call in at Clare's on the way home, maybe stay the night there. She needed to see someone calm and normal before the madness of the inner-city surgery kicked in.

It was not unusual for Clare's house to be in darkness, as the boys tended to watch TV in the dark in the front room while Clare would be online in her bedroom, lit by the fish tank and a novelty object that looked like a fountain and changed colour.

One of two indistinguishable male slacker flatmates answered the door and shouted up for Clare.

"She can't hear," he concluded when there was no response. "She's up there, go on up."

Drew passed the living room where the other flatmate sat in front of a copshow. She headed up the stairs of the grubby old house, eager to reach the sanctuary of Clare's room. It was empty but the computer was on with the email program open onscreen.

Although the scientific part of her brain was screaming Nooooo!, the nosy part obliged Drew to sit down at the machine and scan the inbox. There was an awful lot of mail from Joss. There was mail from Joss unopened, dated five minutes ago, with the subject line "Your sweet girlf". Drew's blood rushed to her face and her hand was shaking as she clicked on the email.

She read: "Hey you! Your girlie was just here, being nice to me. But do I deserve it, I ask myself? ..."

"What the fuck?" The voice came from the door, where her blonde lover stood rigid in an untied dressing gown, her full breasts glowing pink and then green as the novelty light changed hue.

"What's going on?" asked Drew, turning back to the screen.

"You tell me." Clare rushed to the desk and pushed roughly between Drew and the screen. "What are you doing looking at my stuff while I'm in the bathroom? You didn't even say you were here."

"No, and if I had, I wouldn't have seen your 'stuff', would I? Why would Joss be mailing you about me, after she's gone to bed?"

"It's none of your fucking business. What are you doing?"

"That tack isn't getting you anywhere. You can see what I'm doing: I'm reading your emails. And it would be better if I wasn't, wouldn't it?"

She didn't have time to register the raised hand before Clare had slapped her across the face.

"Hey!" Drew tried to push her attacker away.

"Fuck you!" With the words came a blow to the head that knocked the doctor out of her chair.

She screamed and looked up in horror as Clare – face twisted in fury – raised her bare foot. Grabbing it, Drew brought her down to the floor where they battled for supremacy.

A wolf-whistle halted the fight. "Hey! It's my lucky night!" One of the boys was at the bedroom door. "Free lesbo wrestling. And in open robes!"

Private chat 5

Now it's getting tough. See, Amy wants Joss real bad. She has told her that – but then, they have told each other plenty of things in the heat of passion that are just meant to be part of the "scene". Imagine if Amy had fallen for every cyberbutch who said "I'm falling in love with you" or "Now you're mine".

But it's bubbling away in her head so fierce and hot, like a real-life developing relationship that you have to keep secret, like an affair. Because how could she talk about this with Terri, or with Lourdes? They are going to call her one crazy chick.

In a way it's up to Joss now. Joss is the one who has something to lose. If Joss wants to go for it, Amy will get down to JFK and wait with open arms. But she mustn't say so.

<amy~> soooo, you gonna change your handle?
<CustardSlice> Why?
<amy~> I wanna read your name when u talk to me. for god's sake, it says CUSTARDSLICE here!!!
<CustardSlice> God, all right. Wait there.

CustardSlice has left private chat or is ignoring you

<Slice'o'Joss> Happy babe?

<amy~> LOL! happy

<Slice'o'Joss> I wish you were here to tell me that. Curled up next to me. I miss you.

<amy~> woah girl

<Slice'o'Joss> Woah why? I want you here.

<amy~> don't say that unless u mean it

<Slice'o'Joss> I mean it.

<amy~> in real life or in cyber?

<Slice'o'Joss> I MEAN IT

<amy~> in RL or in cyber?

<Slice'o'Joss> FUCK IT AMY, IN REAL FUCKING LIFE

<amy~> O FUCKING K

<Slice'o'Joss> Sorry :)

<amy~> NO NEED TO BE BABE :)

<Slice'o'Joss> Shit shit shit.

<amy~> y'know if this is causing you pain then we can stop

<Slice'o'Joss> What?

<amy~> it's meant to be fun. remember?

<Slice'o'Joss> I can't help it. Don't tell me you don't feel like this.

<amy~> what? crazy?

<Slice'o'Joss> yes

<amy~> yes

<Slice'o'Joss> YES

<amy~> YES YES YES

<Slice'o'Joss> YES YES YES YES YES YESSSSSS

And so on. And where do they go from there?

6
alt

Land of ice

"I'm studying it at university, in the evenings," she said, as we sat upright in the stiff Swedish armchairs in her front room. "How can you not know that?"

"What?"

Jennifer screamed a wordless, old-fashioned scream.

"What?" I asked again, desperate for a clue. "What?"

She shouted at me: "I am studying vulcanology! In an extramural class! On Monday nights! What did you think I did on Monday nights?"

"Er... yoga."

"Why did you think that?"

"Because that *is* what you do, I mean, what you used to do. You said so!"

"Right. For two weeks when Mel first started teaching. Before I realised I didn't like being taught by a friend in my own home. Because it felt weird. Which I told you. At the time. Like I told you I had enrolled on a course."

She was still speaking staccato, breathing heavily in between sentences as she tried to calm herself, and I found it disconcerting. I was certainly very in the wrong now. But how had this happened? Surely if she had told me she was doing an evening class, I would know about it?

"But..." I ventured.

"But what?" she snarled.

"But you never talk about it."

"Well, clearly you haven't heard me talk about it, which is not quite the same thing, is it?"

This explained why her new acquaintances had names like Professor Davis...

It also shed new light on our holiday in Iceland – the worst two weeks we'd had in a long time. I should have seen it coming. The place is called Iceland, for God's sake. What did I think would go on there? Fiery passions? They do have volcanoes, they do call themselves the land of *fire* and ice, but basically it is a cold country consisting of great expanses of barren black earth, volcano dust, and mountains, all different colours. There is nowhere to eat, outside Reykjavik – and we left Reykjavik just two days into the holiday and were not to return there till the very end.

The first place we went had a "summer hotel" which was a school for the rest of the year. Dinner cost around £30 a head. On the first night, we ate the dinner, which was a piece of deer meat and some frozen carrots. I think there may have been a starter that wasn't nice, involving lettuce. Wine was extra. There were no shops in this place, just a waterfall, but we had provisions in our bag so the next night we cooked flavoured noodles in a sandwich box in our room using a plug-in travel element. We were pleased with ourselves for beating the system. This was, what, four days into the holiday. The rain had not stopped all day and even our full waterproofs were not enough to let us go out walking, which is Jennifer's favourite activity. The main reason we had come to Iceland was that she wanted to look at volcanoes and learn more about them. Ever since her first trip to Lanzarote, she was like a kid doing a project for school about volcanoes, cutting things out of the newspapers and taping programmes. (Ah yes, that makes more sense now, doesn't it? Presumably she had enrolled for her diploma.)

Well, I didn't like our little room with its twin beds, it was reminiscent of the hall of residence at university, brick-walled and cell-like. I anticipated two weeks of nasty brick halls and rain. So I went down to the payphone with the guidebook and called the ferry company to see if it was possible to get a boat to the Scottish islands straight away. It was possible but it would take a week to get to Orkney, stopping off at the Faroes. Given that I am prone to seasickness, it didn't seem that clever an idea. The woman was very sympathetic to my plight though, with her gentle Scottish laugh and straightforward advice. I felt a certain intimacy building between us before my phonecard ran out.

Oh, it was beautiful in Iceland, don't get me wrong, it's not that I can't see beauty when it's there before my eyes. But it was a bleak and miserable beauty and it looked at times like a portrayal of my own inner state.

The worst of it came when we stayed in a bunkhouse on a farm in the national park. Jennifer was in her element, surrounded by volcanoes and glaciers, booking herself in for all-day guided walks with crampons. But I was being taken over by the pain of depression. On the first night, I bent over her bunk to have a hug before bed but she was reading and just said "goodnight", looking up for only a second. I reeled away into the bathroom where the tears came. I looked at myself in the mirror and wondered what it would be like to die there, in that bathroom, where the lock on the door didn't work. I would have to use the razor that the big loud German man had left on the sink or the painkillers that his wife had in her open washbag. Everything else was in the dorm itself (including my Swiss army knife which had been proven to cut deep into human flesh before you could say "ouch") and going back out was not an option, with tears streaming down my face and my mouth fixed in a wide open rictus like a newspaper photo of a mother at the funeral of her murdered son. And what was wrong with me? *I wasn't enjoying my holiday.* Not on quite the same scale, in theory, but if we could measure the intensity of feeling, I don't think it would be far off. It's shaming to write that, to suggest that my own pain about nothing is as severe as someone else's pain about something big, and maybe it just means I have no fucking idea about anything. But I like to think it means that I have a very good idea about pain, that I can recognise and understand it in others and that this is a useful skill in the world.

Back to the bathroom, though. I didn't want Jennifer to find me dead; it would spoil her holiday. So I left the bathroom with a towel over my head so no one could see I was crying and threw myself up the wooden ladder on to my bunk. From there, my face was close to a small window that looked out on a hill. Not a distant hill, but the hill the hut was built into. Just there, next to us: side of hill. The front of the hut was better. You walked out of the door and you were high up, looking out across miles of mudflats in front and a circle of mountains topped with ice behind. The sky was low and enormous, full of the gods. You had to walk along a path to the kitchen which was in another shed – they were all wooden buildings made of planks – and on the way you were looking towards the sunset. One night it was stripes of silver.

Some people would have been inspired by this place. In fact we met a woman who said it was her spiritual home and she felt closer to the earth goddess here than anywhere else in the world. I had the impression she had been to a lot of places in the world. For me, it was a kind of hell. I lay on the top bunk that night and even as I felt the pain bursting and spilling from my heart to the rest of my body, even as I felt so desperate that I did not believe I could get through the night, even so I was thinking quite rationally about the nature of depression and how bad it would have to be before I slashed my wrists. I guess suicide is not in my nature or I would have done it that night, which I will always remember as the worst night of my life – until something worse happens. I'm crying now just writing about it, but the pain is absent, thank God.

Jennifer had no idea and I can't ever forgive her for that. The wall between us was so clear to me on that holiday, and that was part of what was making me so desperate. I had asked her, when we were still in the capital with its dinky mini-Amsterdam streets, whether she wanted to try to put things right between us. I suggested we make a commitment to each other while we were away: exchanging rings or just a kiss on a mountaintop, something to say that we wanted to be together. She couldn't do it. She cried as she told me that she couldn't commit to such a miserable, draining person. Admittedly I had cried a lot in the first 24 hours of the holiday and was not at my most attractive, but that was because everything was totally shit between us. She was ready to get into the "interior" of the country and climb up the volcanoes. Having a conversation in which we agreed not to commit to each other did not appear to mar her enjoyment.

The morning after my near-suicide in the country bunkhouse, she was similarly unconcerned. She had reached up to pat my bed when she noticed it was shaking with grief, but then she had gone to sleep, and in the morning it was a good hour before she asked, "What was up with you last night?" I just shook my head. I couldn't go back there.

A way to be happy

Books you should not let yourself read if you are trying to think of reasons not to leave your girlfriend, especially if you are inclined to relate to a male narrator: *The Night Listener* by Armistead Maupin, *Intimacy* by Hanif Kureishi, that book with the faces cut out, can't remember what it's called, I threw it out the window one night and it wasn't there in the morning.* I read this story in which they go away to a dream island holiday and they still don't have sex, etc etc. Honestly, I could have been reading about the two of us.

I was almost in tears when a booming male voice from the street invaded my thoughts, telling a tale about women being murdered in the shop under my flat. There were occasional inter-jections from a young woman. Frustratingly, the voice kept boom-ing but I could only hear about every third word, as the traffic cut across his speech. I pulled open the curtains, expecting to look down on some old eccentric who was boring the tits off a stranger. Instead, I saw a crowd of people facing my house and a man giv-ing a talk to them: a guided walk, lit orange by the street lamp.

I threw the book out of the window (which provoked posh gasps, shrieks and laughter) and went into this crying that was not about being moved by the story I'd read or upset by the one I'd heard. It was like a hole opened up inside me, or the thin covering that was hiding the hole peeled back, and out of the hole came the frightening lonely sadness and desperation. Given what had happened in Iceland, I now thought of it as "being suicidal without the killing yourself bit". I had been told that the killing yourself bit was a consolation – knowing that one day you would go ahead and kill yourself, that when the pain was bad enough you could kill yourself – it made it better. And I didn't even have that.

Of course, you don't get much more self-indulgent than that, crying about your relationship not being exactly how you want it, crying about not wanting to kill yourself, envying people who want to kill themselves, well you can't go on all your life like that, can you? And yet that was exactly what I had been doing. All my fucking life.

And now I had this way out, a way to be happy and stop crying. If someone really loved me and was able to show it physically and constantly, then I would stop being depressed. And that was what could happen. I just had to start going out with Amy, and stop going out with Jennifer. I probably only had to tell Jennifer that I was fascinated by someone else and then she would finish with me or I would finish with her, depending on how that particular conversation panned out.

Then I would go and live in Greenwich Village or the meat-packing district or the garment district, or next to the Chrysler Building or in Queens or The Bronx. My hazy virtual geography of the city had been built up over a lifetime of armchair Ameriphilia. I couldn't listen to Simon and Garfunkel's patter between songs at The Concert in Central Park without being transported, stoned, to a balmy Central Park. And I wasn't a Mancunian London Jew when I watched Woody Allen, but a member of the same diaspora, at the next table in the same deli. So what if I'd never been there? I'd been there.

11.45pm. I printed off a colour map of New York from the internet before meeting up with Amy.

* *Sam the Cat* by Matthew Klam

Private chat 6

<Slice'o'Joss> I haven't stopped thinking about last night.

<amy~> me either

<Slice'o'Joss> Amy.

<amy~> that's my name

<Slice'o'Joss> Amy...

<amy~> uh-huh

<Slice'o'Joss> Where do you live?

<amy~> have you had a bang to the head hon and forgotten?

<Slice'o'Joss> Where exactly?

<amy~> park slope. does that help??

<Slice'o'Joss> Insufficient data

<amy~> brooklyn

<Slice'o'Joss> I'm looking on my map...

<amy~> oh my! reeeesearch! u is keen babe

<Slice'o'Joss> I see Brooklyn...

<amy~> see stirling place tween 6th & 7th aves?

<Slice'o'Joss> K!! :) I like it there.

<amy~> me too. u should see my apartment tonight. my panties are drying everywhere

<Slice'o'Joss> Hmmm, looking good. Wish I was there.

\<amy~\> u r here babe. here with me.

\<Slice'o'Joss\> Will u call me?

\<amy~\> what??

\<Slice'o'Joss\> OK, never mind.

\<amy~\> where did that come from?

\<Slice'o'Joss\> Sorry, sorry.

\<amy~\> no i'm sorry

\<Slice'o'Joss\> Shit.

\<amy~\> hey it's ok babe

\<amy~\> u surprised me

\<Slice'o'Joss\> I'll never say it again.

\<amy~\> why not?

\<Slice'o'Joss\> Now I'm confused.

\<amy~\> where did it come from though?

\<Slice'o'Joss\> From my heart.

\<amy~\> oh hon. what do u want? what's happening there in london?

\<Slice'o'Joss\> Nothing. Absolutely nothing.

Intimacy junkie

I was an intimacy junkie. And now that I had realised it, my entire life made sense. Why did Pascale and I break up all those years ago? Because my new connection with someone called Ellen was drawing me so strongly that it was all I could do to wait till I'd got her alone before I pushed my fingers into her cunt. Hm. That's soooo romantic. And then KABOOM! I'm way surprised that Pascale doesn't want to stay with me after I tell her that I've slept with Ellen and can't promise not to do it again. Yes sireeee, that is what I said to her, word for goddam word. No, turns out that Pacale doesn't want to be with me any more 'cos she wants to be with this witchy woman we know. Once, when we were all out on a walk together, the witchy woman bent to pick up a worm from the pavement and throw it over a wall so it wouldn't get trodden on. Later, when Pascale was in love with her and had gone to her house for the night, when I phoned the house in desperation and Pascale came to the phone all giggly and told me not to be silly, then I wondered whether the worm was symbolic. Was I that worm? Had I been trodden on or tossed to safety? Or was Pascale the worm?

Either way, it's not like I didn't know what could happen. In fact, as I had recently said to Amy (who was suitably offended), all it took was for a nice femme to come on to me with the old tricks – e.g. smiling while stretching the neck coquettishly, or in the case of the chatroom, calling me "you poor old thing" or "sir" – and I was hers for life, whether she wanted me or not or was just flirting in that self-contained way, that gameplan way that femmes have. It was like, "Oh, look at that butch, I think I'll go and make her want me before I check out the canapes" (modishly pronounced "k'nayps", *comme* "kneidlach").

Sometimes it's hard to tell what is real and what is generated by my own mind, in any of its many states, including normal, manic, depressed, and altered by cannabis. In fact, most of the time, I just don't know. Do you? Do you really know what is real? How can you tell? There should be a test for it. They can send men to the moon (allegedly) and make sanitary towels so thin you can't see them, but they can't test whether something is real or not. Even the test for lying, which of course is a different thing again, is not conclusive. It works on *Rikki Lake* but not necessarily in court. I should check my facts there. That's the trouble with telling a story. Some of it you can remember, some of it you can make up, some of it you should not make up because of the responsibility to the reader.

See, this is it, this is the manic state. You would not believe the speed at which I am typing this now. The thoughts are leaping from topic to topic but my fingers just keep right on moving like there are no seams. That is because I was educated in the art of touch-typing at the expense of the great British tax-payer, Lord love her.

I was on the dole and it was a government scheme. They had noticed I was a graduate and they felt unable to give me any further training that might make me more employable – until they realised I couldn't type.

The class was held in a day centre for the unemployable. This was under the Tories. Using electic typewriters, women and men with challenges ranging from mild learning difficulties to fragrancy issues were slowly practising an exercise from the teacher. I asked if I had to join this particular class, which built over a year to a cert-ificate in office skills, including filing alphabetically, answering the telephone and writing a letter. And because I spoke in a particular way to them, I was allowed to sit by myself, just like in playgroup or in infants' school. I sat at a computer that had a self-teach pro-gram on it and I learnt to touch-type in a few days, after which I stopped going to the scheme and they kept paying me the £10 a week on top of my dole because they didn't want to admit they'd lost a trainee or to add me back on to the statistics.

OK, so now I can touch-type. My mother always told me not to learn because I would wind up typing letters for other people but that has not happened, luckily. I am not the most accurate typist but when I have something to say, I can get it down, and in email and in the chatrooms, that's what matters. Quick, clear, witty. That's it. That's the girl bagged. That's the other side of the smile and the coquettish neck. If you had to sum up butch/femme in a few words, that would do it. Of course, the femme could just as well do the quick, clear, witty, but the point is that she doesn't have to. If she chooses, she can just wink or look across the room. It's her call.

So how did I get in this mess? I kept asking myself. I had been encouraging Jennifer to open up to me and she was doing so, app-roximately every six weeks. I am trying not to be crude here. When I say open up, I mean to speak honestly to me. But while we're on the subject, there was also the little matter of sex, which was not going fantastically well. She seldom initiated it, and when we did fuck, the effort expended was not exactly equal on both sides. I would say it was around 90:10. She had not gone down on me in about two years. I remembered the last time because after a minute she moved her mouth to my lower belly and started kissing it in a manner so uncharacteristic that I could only conclude she had not been enjoying the earlier activity. I didn't want to know why, just then. I shoved her out the way and wanked myself to climax. Maybe not everyone concluded their love-making in this manner but it stopped both parties from getting bored and irritable.

If we were really having a tough time then we could just have broken up. But we were close and distant simultaneously, while the lure of intimacy with others grew more intense. I knew that Drew thought I was mad to consider meeting up with Amy, but she didn't understand the nature of our relationship. Already it was an affair. Of course, no one would have divorced me over it. Jennifer would not have thought it was an affair, seeing as I was thousands of miles from Amy. No, she would have thought it was a waste of time. I did tell her that I sometimes went in the dyke chatrooms, but she didn't rise to the bait. Then, when we were with some friends who were talking about cybersex, she turned to me with new interest and a little fear and asked, "Do you do that?" and I said, nervously, "Sometimes." She laughed at me. "You poor old thing," she said, "not getting enough. I must do better." And the others pretended not to hear.

Of course, we did talk about the fact that we were having less sex. Or rather, I talked about it. She seemed to think it was a natural shift in a long-term relationship, even clipping articles on bed-death from *Diva*, whereas I felt rather differently.

"It's the closest, most intimate thing you can do with another human being," I insisted, like a PSE teacher or the counsellor off *South Park*.

"What about squeezing spots?" she countered.

"Jen! Please! This is important."

She laughed. "All right, sorry."

"Sex is special, we save it for each other and no one else, and what's the point of that if we don't *have* it with each other?"

"We do!"

"Not very often."

"Maybe you should go and have it with someone else then," she suggested.

I looked to see if she was serious. "You'd like that, would you?" I asked. "If I was sleeping around?"

"I wouldn't have to know, would I?"

I was stunned. "How did we get to this? You used to be so... keen."

"Relationships change, Joss. When we first got together, I was in love with you and that was all that mattered. But that was a long time ago, before we knew what was wrong with each other. It doesn't stay like that."

"What do you mean, 'wrong with each other'? What's wrong with me? Have you had enough of me? Are you hoping I'll go off with someone else if I start sleeping around?" She did not interrupt with reassurances, so I continued. "Or maybe there's someone else *you'd* like to fuck and that's why you're looking into polyamory?" I spat out this last word.

"Do we have to talk about this now?" she asked.

We were sitting in her living room and I sensed she was uncomfortable at having a private conversation in a potentially shared space.

"Why? There's no one else downstairs, is there?"

"I think Mel's in the garage... and her mother's in the en suite bathroom."

"I thought her mother had left?"

"It's a long story. She might have to live here forever."

"Right. But neither of them can actually hear us discussing our relationship – which we're actually entitled to discuss between ourselves as far as I know – can they?"

"No, *actually*, they probably can't."

"What?"

"What what?"

"What's that 'actually'?"

"Just what you say all the time when you're irritated with me. *Actually* this and *actually* that."

"Oh, sorry! God forbid I should use the same word more than once. But if I could return to the matter in hand..." I sighed and said it. "Have you gone off me?"

"No! ... I told you, I don't want to talk about it now. Where's the remote?"

I picked it up off the floor and threw it at her. It was supposed to fly over her shoulder but it smacked her on the forehead and the evening degenerated.

What the makeover maestro sees

Well, it's done, but it is not his greatest work. Not something he will be remembered for in years to come. The girl keeps asking if he is going to take away some of the furniture and he can see her point, to be fair, because there is rather a lot of it. He's not sure she's happy, as such, but they rarely are, these days – think they know it all because they've seen it on TV.

Still, she smiles sweetly enough for the camera. Pierre (late and slow, as per) has snapped her sitting on the pink chair and drinking tea on the pink bed and so on, when suddenly she's screaming like a bloody maniac, blood-curdling screams that bring the bulldyke from the next room (who supposedly works for *MI* but is at home all day every day watching television).

The girl's only seen a bloody mouse! They have to catch it for her in a dented saucepan while she stands screaming on the bed. Pierre seems to think himself clever for throwing the lidded pan out of the window.

Talk about a decline in the standard of the homes. And as for the morals of the occupants… Well, Pierre has met his match. When he lies down on the bed next to her "to get a better shot", everyone's suspicions are confirmed.

Perhaps seeing how this looks, he gets up and says, "I need a few more shots for back-up, Lance. You and Camilla needn't wait around, though – it must have been a long day for you."

"Not as long as yours is going to be, dear," he is tempted to reply.

It will be hard to keep this from Kitty. And if past record is anything to go by, there'll be a new "assistant" on Pierre's invoices by the end of the month.

Letter from America

With the dearth of sex in my primary relationship, I was turning into one of those people (usually male in the myths) who think about it every thirty seconds. That's a sure sign of a manic episode. Perhaps a little structure might have helped but Drew did not think it was a good idea for me to go back to work before I felt "normal". That could take some time. A mouse had been sighted next door, in Madam's bizarre pink room, and I was rodent-nervy all over again. But my neighbour had more sizeable matters than mice on her mind.

"I've got a job!" she told me delightedly when the makeover was complete. "It's because I've got such a good sense of interiors. The photographer wants me to work for him! In magazines!"

He was back the next night to bonk her, which did not help me keep my mind off sex. Luckily I had some displacement activities saved up from previous bouts of mania (bouts during which, traditionally, an artist would paint as an outlet for the energy, if she had a creative synapse left in her brain). For instance, I could play an old Proclaimers tape very loud and dance wildly to it on the bed. I could play Paperboy on my old B&W Gameboy, bought with a tax rebate when they first came on the market, then stashed away after it became clear that neither Pascale nor myself could lead a normal life with it – she played Tetris all evening without looking up, barring a break to take a pee or a Mars Bar; I took Super Mario to a new level each night while she slept. But now I had dusted it off and found it to be eminently playable in my bedsit by day or by night. And I could rent videos of TV comedies from Archway Library. It only cost £2 for the whole series of *The Royle Family* for a week.

But in between these time-fillers, I had to relieve the sexual tension that was my life. I might watch two episodes of the Royles and then have a wank, or play Paperboy for two hours and then get high and then get naked. I might get into bed with a dildo and a can of Coke and a tape of last week's *Eurotrash*, wound to a table-dancing segment...

I had to tell you enough to get the idea but I may have crossed a line there, sorry.

The rules of narrative – nay, the laws of the jungle and the street and the dyke bar – stated that it was only a matter of time before I took Jen at her word and slept with someone else, or fucked someone else from behind with my hands on her tits, to be precise.

I was still flirting with Clare by email, while promising myself I would never shag my best friend's girlfriend (even though this kind of behaviour has long been fashionable in my circles). But the more I flirted, the more I thought of her in That Way. And in the end, I went back to work mainly to see her.

In a new tradition that had started while I was off sick (she called it "keeping you in touch with the office"), Clare was including bits in her email of an evening, or even of a morning, that encouraged me to fantasise about getting off together at work. One particular passage about the office toilets was the most explicit. And it was both a shock and an inevitability when she followed me into the toilets in real life (or RL as the cyberbuffs call it) to whisper her fantasy from the next cubicle. Was she masturbating? I flushed, threw open the door, ran from the loos in terror.

If we bumped into each other unexpectedly, we could barely contain ourselves. In the kitchen, she dropped her Tomato Flavour Drink while removing it from the hatch of the machine. Red water spilled across the floor while we stared at it in silence. At the fax machine, I was so flustered to find her waiting behind me that I had to ask for her help in sending a reply to a fax from Simon & Schuster, New York. (Later, with insufficient work to do, I looked up their address, Avenue of the Americas, on that map on the internet. It was in Manhattan. Amy was in Brooklyn. I looked up the subway links. And that was another problem: if I wasn't thinking about Clare, I was thinking about Amy.)

Private chat 7

Amy has spent quite some time considering their last date. "Call me" is not an instruction she has ever followed when it was given to her by a cyberbutch. She avoids the chatrooms called Phone Fun for precisely the same reason: she does not want them to have her number to call whenever they want, and she does not want to call them because why the hell should she, when they take her so effectively online? Phone sex is lazy. They only have to talk. Or grunt.

This is different, of course, and it's not like she didn't expect it to come around – not like she wasn't hoping that Joss would say those words some time soon. Call me. Call me.

Since then they have exchanged emails. Amy cares enough that she is not going to push Joss where she doesn't want to go. But who was it who raised the goddam topic? Amy has been so cautious for so long, it feels like she is holding herself in, just when she wants to give herself up. And now it's seven o'clock.

<Slice'o'Joss> Hi there babe.
<amy~> hi
<Slice'o'Joss> Amy I'm nervous.

<amy~> and me

<Slice'o'Joss> I don't know what happens next

<amy~> u don't have to know

<Slice'o'Joss> You're not angry with me for... anything?

<amy~> no babe. god no

<Slice'o'Joss> Come here, I have to kiss you.

<amy~> mmm. here i am for you to kiss

<Slice'o'Joss> mmmm <kissing u>

<amy~> kissing u back. u feel good

<Slice'o'Joss> I love your lips. Ready for me.

<amy~> they all are

<Slice'o'Joss> :) Naughty

<amy~> that's what u like

<Slice'o'Joss> That is what I like. I like you. I want you

<amy~> i'm right here babe

<Slice'o'Joss> I have to ask you something

<amy~> go

<Slice'o'Joss> When I said that thing...

<amy~> we've discussed this

<Slice'o'Joss> But you haven't answered, not really

<amy~> what have u told yr gf?

[pause]

<amy~> ???

[pause]

<amy~> i'm waiting babe

<Slice'o'Joss> Sorry. I'm thinking what to say

<amy~> OK don't rush

<Slice'o'Joss> She knows I do cyber. She doesn't know about *you*.

<amy~> so what ru doing?

<amy~> u gonna be my slice'o'joss forever? u can only spare
a slice?

<Slice'o'Joss> I don't know. I don't know. I can't talk about it like
this. I have to speak to you. Please babe.

<amy~> mmm. a butch who begs

<Slice'o'Joss> God don't tease me you bitch.

<amy~> hey hey, gimme the number hon

<Slice'o'Joss> ???

<amy~> gimme the fuckin number. and it better not start 555.

A lot can happen in bed

I was in bed with the laptop. I had given her my mobile number because the landline was tied up with the internet. I don't know when I was last this excited. There was an inexorability to it but I didn't know if I would be able to speak when she did ring, if I would be able to turn the phone on and take the call like a normal person. My fingers were hovering over the keyboard, wondering whether to type any encouragement, then over the phone, waiting for something more useful to touch. They were damp with expectation. What now? What was I doing now? And then it rang.

I picked it up from the bedside table. The screen was lit up green in the dark room. Instead of "CALLER UNKNOWN", it displayed a single word: CLARE.

There was a roar in my head of colour and noise, like the essence of a migraine captured as the soundtrack for a violent movie. I dashed the phone to the floor where it broke into four pieces.

Clare was Amy.

How the fuck was that possible? And yet... everything Ali had told me should have prepared me for precisely this eventuality. JESUS. JEEEEZUS. How had I let it happen?

I felt sick. I had discussed Amy more than once with Clare. What had I said? It didn't matter. Whatever I had said, she must have loved every moment. Christ, she had given me advice, told me at one point to go slow, told me another time to go with my feelings. Jesus. All that time, she was laughing her mad head off.

I needed to speak to Jen, lovely straightforward Jen, but I couldn't phone so late at night for fear of waking Mel's precious mother, so I would just have to turn up unannounced. I bumped my bike down the stairs to the street and took off. The air on my face as I free-wheeled down Highgate Hill made me cry out for the love of life.

It took ten minutes to get to Jen's. The house was in darkness but I let myself in and climbed the stairs blindly.

I opened the door to Jen's room. I had not seen it in candlelight in the last three years and I took a moment to adjust to the glow.

"Mother?" It was Melanie's voice. She was lying in Jennifer's bed. When she saw it was not Ma but me, her expression changed two or three times, settling on something between smugness and evil.

"Where's Jennifer?" I asked.

With the timing of a magician, Melanie whipped back the duvet to reveal my girlfriend, doing what, for her, did not come naturally. And more worrying still, she didn't stop.

Rebel Rebel

Clare had some news for me when I arrived at the office. You'd think that, even if last night had somehow been erased from her memory while she slept, she might have been sensitive to the state I was in, but apparently my pink eyes, puffy face and bike-oiled jeans were invisible to a receptionist of her zippy disposition. She psst at me and widened her eyes in a mimeshow of urgent and thrilling revelation-to-come. Presumably the presence of Caroline Chatterby, whose den she guarded, prevented audible speech.

I walked past her blankly to my workstation but there was no one at the subs' desk and only one person in the artroom – Geoff looking bemused. It was 10.30.

"Where is everyone?" he asked me.

"I was about to ask you that," I replied before retracing my weary steps and allowing Clare to shepherd me to the lift and thence to the fuggy smoking room, the least private space in The Tower but the one universally chosen for the unburdening of secrets by those who fancied themselves as rebels. And, as it transpired, that was exactly how Clare fancied herself.

"I'm going to rebel," she told me, having taken a long drag on her Silk Cut Blue Straw. The room, for once, was empty.

"Why are you putting the emphasis on the first syllable?" I asked. "The verb is re-*bel*, the noun is *reb*-el."

"I'm going to the noun," she said. "Rebel – the company."

"Erm…?"

"The new magazine company? Formed by people who've left Magazineland?" She clearly couldn't decide whether to be thrilled or frustrated that I was sooo outcrowd that I didn't know what she was talking about.

"Where do you *think* everyone's *gone*, Joss?"

"I thought they might be attending the cremation of my union with Jennifer."

"What?"

"We broke up last night."

"Because of you and me?"

"You wish."

"Well why then?"

"Oh, don't let me hold you up. You're going to Rebel, apparently. With everyone except me and Geoff."

"Yeah. Do you want a job?"

"Oh. Oh-hoh. This is rich. Do *I* want a job? What, *you'll* get *me* a job? Do you know how long I've worked in magazines? I think I can get my own job. Actually, I think I've got a job. As far as I know, the editor's still here. Isn't she?"

"Yeah. That's why I came in. I need a reference."

"You what? I thought you'd just been headhunted."

She looked at the opposite wall, where a poster for *Wallet* showed a generic naked lady.

"I'm going to be PA to the editor of a new magazine called *Diamond Gaff*. But because I haven't been here very long they wanted a reference and I can't ask the agency because of… Well, I can't ask them."

I could think of a few reasons, in fact, why the last temping agency might not give her a reference: fabricating her CV and then slapping the person who found out, for instance; or sleeping with two of the clients on alternate nights over several months while telling each of them that she was monogamous. But I couldn't dwell on the facts of Clare's scary history, as detailed by Ali. My mind was too busy rifling through recent files in the Unexplained cabinet... The chief sub they called e-Tim, whispering on the phone instead of using email... the entire features department going out to lunch in one place at once, and Kitty and Trixie later seen looking at a magazine together... Oh God, I'd heard people talking in the lift, "He's going to revel," and "She took a call from Beryl" – as I thought. What did I think they were talking about? Nothing, I didn't think it was anything to do with me. Why hadn't I asked anyone what was going on? Why hadn't they told me? Why why why...

"Jesus H Fucking Christ!" I exclaimed.

"What?" Clare had to close her mouth before saying this – she must have been talking.

"Somebody said to me last week... somebody, who was it? Somebody taller than me... They said, 'Are you going to Rebel?' and I said, 'I don't know, when is it?' *When is it!* For fuck's sake."

Clare started to laugh. "Well, it does sound like a club."

"Never mind sounding like, it *is* a club – it's a club I haven't been asked to join. Christ... Hannah!"

Clare looked back at the naked lady. I walked out and took the lift to *The Outside Room*. There was no one there.

I went down to the Kwikeetz and there was Clare, buying a banana and a bottle of chocolate milk.

"Don't you want to say anything to me about last night?"

I asked on impulse, in the kind of stage whisper favoured by Jennifer.

She looked at me, searching my face as if she could find the right answer there. Then she took a stab at it: "Er... sorry?"

"Sorry for what?"

"About you and Jennifer?"

"Try again."

"What? Oh, the phonecall! I wanted to tell you everything..."

"Next please!" called the man at the till, and Clare broke our gaze and trotted up to him with a merry greeting. Perhaps she actually had a dual personality.

Back at my desk, I checked my email. For the first time in my Magland life, there was none.

Geoff came over. "They've blocked it while they try to read all the traffic between Rebel and Magazineland."

"What, they're reading people's mail? How do you know?"

"Colin just told me. He said everyone in IT has been deployed to find evidence against Lucretia or whatever her name is." He flicked back his hair. "I might go up there actually. There might be a job for me."

"How come?"

"Oh, I used to do some hacking and I've kept pretty up to date."

"Right. Go up there then, Geoff. I'd hate you to feel you had to stay for my sake." Perhaps I forgot to put the sarcasm into my voice before it left my mouth, I don't know. But he nodded solemnly, wished me luck, shook my hand, and left.

I checked my home email instead, the web version which takes forever to load. There were three messages: Tim, Hannah and "Amy".

I scanned Tim's while I steadied myself for what was to come.

"Hi Joss! Sorry, we've all gone to Rebel. Didn't want to hassle you with all this after your stress thing, so thought we'd leave you to it. Don't let the buggers etc. Lunch soon? Tim."

Then I double-clicked on "Amy".

"Babe, what happened? u wanted me to call!? hon, write me!! it's gonna be ok. isn't it? i hope you're ok. shit, what happened? ~ A ~ xxxxx"

I logged off and rested my head on the desk. As there were now only three of us left in the offices amid the unanswered phones, I could hear every move up the other end, reverberating through the desk. It was oddly comforting, reminiscent of story-time in primary school. I heard Clare ask Caroline if she had a minute, go into her room and shut the door. I heard Clare leave before lunchtime. And I heard Caroline's noisy aura as she worked her way towards the rest of us, that is, towards me. I reckoned I had twenty seconds to prepare but I wasn't sure what to prepare for. I sat up.

And then she was there, standing on the other side of the low barrier that designated the edge of the subs' desk, looking me straight in the eye.

And she said these words: "You touch-type, don't you?"

Rebel drains Magland

An estimated two hundred editorial, sales and administrative staff moved from Magazineland to Lavinia Buff-Jones's new company Rebel in just 48 hours this week.

Buff-Jones, who spent five years with the media giant before setting up on her own in a secret deal with venture capitalists, denies claims from her former bosses that she "deliberately ran down top titles" in her position as publishing director in the months prior to her departure.

She counters that she repositioned failing homes titles such as *Modern Interiors* to gain a greater share of the market but became disillusioned by a lack of support from above.

"In the end I realised I would be better off with my own company, focused on the magazines of the future," she says.

The management at Magazineland, where shares plummeted on Wednesday from 210p to 170p, has declined to comment further on the shock exodus.

Those who resigned gave no notice, leaving many magazines with only a skeleton staff.

Insiders believe there are further resignations in store at The Tower as the Covent Garden rival fills more vacancies on launch monthlies including the babies magazine *Sprog City*, youthful homes glossy *Diamond Gaff* and the "anti-health" title *Don't Eat Your Greens*.

Rebel is named after Buff-Jones's pug.

—*UK Press Week*

It's up to you

Anything could have happened next. I could have taken to my bed again, but I'd been there, done that. Clare, having started at the new magazine, could have arranged a makeover for Jen and Melanie in their happy home, with photographs by Pierre, assisted by Madam. I could have sat outside Caroline Chatterby's office typing for the rest of my life, or they could have shut down *Modern Interiors*, or sold it to Rebel with me included in the package, a sitting sub: *Diamond Gaff incorporating Modern Interiors incorporating Joss*.

It's possible that some of these things will happen yet. But I won't be there to see them, because I did something no one believed I was going to do, and I did it with only one witness, my little sis.

Hannah had not left the company. Nor did her job appear to be in any danger (the publisher having stayed put at Magland after a lover's tiff with Buffy). The reason her office was empty on Brain-drain Day was that the small staff of *The Outside Room* were all on an awayday at the printers with a go-karting trip thrown in. When she came back, Hannah took a look at my broken mobile, which is the same model as hers. She showed me how to reactivate it and then I listened to my messages.

She has a beautiful voice, Amy. How could I have doubted? My Amy, my beautiful girl. When I paint her portrait, her voice will light it up.

It's not that expensive to fly to New York on standby. And that's where I'm headed right now. They have individual TV screens in front of each seat on this plane. I'm watching *Mr Bean*.

I haven't told Drew. She hasn't rung for a while and I've left it, because I know what she'll say about everything before she says it. The more she claimed to have the answers, the more I wanted to tell her that her own girlfriend was a pathological liar with a history of violence – but that might not be wise.

I didn't tell Clare I was leaving, either. She's already at Rebel, where they get free chocolate all week and "duvet days", apparently.

Hannah was good. She didn't want me to go; she wanted me to buy a return ticket. But in the end she said she'll come and see me if I stay there. If. I told my mum and dad I'm going for a few weeks. But I didn't say that to Amy. I said, "Amy, hon, I'm coming to be with you." And she said, "What kept you so long?"

She'll be there to meet me at the airport. She'll have her arms out, ready to enfold me. She'll hold me tight. I'll make love to her tonight – in Park Slope, in Brooklyn, New York.

end

New from DIVA Books

Smother
Linda Innes

A dark comedy about the harm we cause each other

Mary has an obsession: to prove her love for Tanya. She will persist no matter what abuse she gets back. But sooner or later, the worm has to turn...

Innes's brilliant first novel, set in the north-east of England, is packed with sharp humour and dark suspense. As the story unfolds, we see how each woman's relationship with her own mother has doomed her adult love affairs. And now, it seems, someone will have to pay.

"This is a hugely enjoyable debut novel; a passionate journey through a landscape of damaged relationships. Innes writes beautifully with a divine eye for detail. This is a powerful new voice, exploring difficult and important territory, and it's immensely readable, too" Julia Darling (author, *Crocodile Soup*)

RRP £8.95   ISBN 1-873741-61-8

DIVA Books are available from all good bookshops, including Borders, Libertas!, Gay's the Word, Silver Moon and Prowler, and branches of Waterstone's.

DIVA also has a mail order service on freephone 0800 45 45 66 (international: +44 20 8340 8644). Please quote the following codes: Smother SMO618, The Touch Typist TOU650. Or go to www.divamag.co.uk